Balancing the Odds

Sam eyed the deserters. This was no dime novel. Five against one was odds he wasn't going to beat. Life was a bitch. With his foot he pushed his chair away from the table.

The five deserters went for their guns. Sam stood, drawing his pistol in the same motion. He cocked it and shot Hastings in the chest. As Hastings went down, Sam crouched and swiveled right to the next man, the one with the forage cap. He fired a fraction of a second before the man fired at him. A hole blossomed in the man's forehead, just under the cap's brim. Bullets were flying around Sam now. He threw himself to the floor as bullets gouged the dirt near his head.

Lying on the floor, his back was to the last two men. They were only feet away. Even as Sam cocked his pistol and rolled over, he knew his luck had run out. . . .

Also by Dale Colter

The Regulator
Diablo at Daybreak
Deadly Justice
Dead Man's Ride
Gravedancer

Published by
HARPERPAPERBACKS

DALE COLTER

THE REGULATOR

THE SCALP HUNTERS

HarperPaperbacks
A Division of HarperCollins*Publishers*

HarperPaperbacks *A Division of* HarperCollins*Publishers*
10 East 53rd Street, New York, N.Y. 10022

Cover art by Miro

First printing: February 1992

Printed in the United States of America

10 9 8 7 6 5 4 3 2 1

CHAPTER 1

MARTIN CRUZ KNEW THAT THE TALL RIDER was trouble from the first moment he saw him.

There was something about the way the man sat his horse—arrogant, challenging. As the man drew closer, the terrible scar which ran down the left side of his face only confirmed Martin's suspicions.

Martin Cruz knew about trouble. His small cantina stood on the edge of the *Jornada del Fuego*, the "Journey of Fire," a hundred-odd miles of sun-blasted sand, rock, and thorn leading to the Eagle Mountains. Martin's well was the last certain water until the mountains were reached. Few travelers came this way, and even fewer came with good intentions—a scattering of unmarked graves behind the cantina gave proof to that. Martin had seen many *mal hombres*, and this man was as bad as any.

The tall man halted his horse in front of the cantina and dismounted. He removed his rifle and saddlebags from his saddle. He raised the well bucket, dipped in the ladle, and took a long drink.

Martin moved forward cheerfully. H was friendly to everyone. That was one of the qualities that had kept him alive so long. *"Buenos dias, señor."*

The tall man had dirty blond hair, worn long, a predatory nose, much broken, and ice-blue eyes—the eyes of a killer. He turned those eyes on Martin. "See to my horse," he said.

"Sí, señor," said Martin.

"Be careful with him," the tall man added. "He's a good animal. He's got a ways to be rode yet."

"Sí, señor. I am very careful, always."

The tall man nodded. As Martin led the horse to the corral, the tall man went into the adobe cantina, ducking his head at the low entrance.

After the harsh brightness of the desert, it took Sam Slater's eyes a moment to become accustomed to the dim light. It was cool inside. There was a musty smell, and a sheen of dust hung in the air, illumined by the shaft of sunlight that slanted through the doorway.

The owner's heavy-breasted wife was behind the bar. "I get some food here?" Sam asked her.

"Sí, sí," the woman replied. *"Frijoles, carne.* I bring. You want something to drink—whiskey, tequila?"

"Cerveza," Sam said. It was too hot for anything else.

The woman went out the back door, to the kitchen.

There was one other customer in the cantina, a boyish-looking, well-dressed fellow in his mid-thirties. He sat in a dark corner, idly laying out cards on the table before him, a bottle of tequila and a dirty glass to one side.

The man flashed Sam an engaging grin. "Afternoon, friend."

Sam nodded.

The man indicated the bottle. "Join me?"

"No, thanks," Sam said.

The man shrugged good-naturedly and went back to his cards.

The owner's wife brought Sam his food and beer. The woman looked part Apache, which was not unnatural. This was Apache country. Probably her Indian blood was the reason the Apaches allowed her and her husband to remain alive, eking out a living on the edge of the *Jornada.*

Sam ate. The food was tasteless, but it filled him up. The best he could say for the beer was that it was wet.

It had taken days of hard travel for Sam to get here, and the worst of his journey was yet to come. Now, he must cross the forbidding *Jornada*, to the Eagle Mountains. Somewhere in those mountains was the stronghold of Thomas Crawford and his gang of scalp hunters. There was five thousand dollars reward for Crawford, five hundred for each member of his gang.

It was a reward Sam Slater intended to collect.

Sam Slater was a bounty hunter. Men called him "The Regulator."

Sam was operating blind. He had no description of Crawford. All he knew about the man was that he was a former Union Army colonel who sold Apache scalps to the Mexican government. The Mexicans had long been plagued by Apache terror. In an effort to reduce the Indian depredations, the governor of Sonora had offered a bounty of fifty dollars for each Apache scalp brought to him. Crawford and his men raided on both sides of the border, killing men, women, and children, selling their scalps. They killed not only Apaches, but peaceful Papagoes, Mexicans—anyone whose hair might pass for that of an Indian. They had become a worse threat to the southwestern frontier than the Apaches.

Sam had reasons other than money for taking on this job—personal reasons. Apaches had taken him in when he was on the run from killing his uncle in Montana—the same uncle who'd given him the fearsome scar on his cheek. Sam had learned all he knew about tracking—and about many other things besides—from the Apaches. He regarded them as his own people, his family. He reckoned he had a few scores to settle for them.

Hoofbeats sounded outside, approaching the cantina. Sam did not look up from his meal. The well-dressed man in the corner poured another drink.

Martin Cruz started for the door. "More travelers. *Gracias a Dios*. The business has never been so good."

Then Martin looked out, and his heart faltered.

There were five men, rough customers, dirty and unshaven. They were mounted on four horses, with one man riding double. They wore bits and pieces of Army uniforms—one had a forage cap, one had sky-blue trousers, one had a blue jacket. Their saddles were Army-issue McClellans, and their horses wore the "U.S." brand. They carried Army Springfield carbines and Colt pistols.

They were deserters, men who hadn't been able to take the strict Army discipline and who had decided to run for it.

They dismounted and tied their horses outside the cantina, then looked at the animals in the corral.

"*B-Buenos dias*," Martin stammered hesitantly.

The men pushed past him without a word and went inside. They looked around. Their leader, a dark-whiskered, sallow fellow, threw some coins on the rough bar top. "Tequila," he told Martin's wife. He pushed back his battered campaign hat, revealing a mass of unkempt hair.

Cruz's wife set five glasses on the bar. She got a bottle and started to pour. The lead deserter grabbed the bottle from her hand. He drank from it and passed it to the next man. They did not return the bottle to Cruz's wife. The men slugged back the harsh liquor, cutting the desert dust in their throats. "Damn, that's good," said the one wearing the forage cap. To the leader, he said, "Here, Hastings, give me some more." He took the bottle and drank.

"So far, so good," said another, wearing a gray, Army-issue shirt. "We're almost home free."

"Almost, but not quite," said the sallow-faced one called Hastings.

Martin had come back from tending the horses, and Hastings turned to him. "That sorrel gelding out back—who's he belong to?"

Martin nodded toward Sam, who continued eating.

Hastings put down the bottle and walked over to Sam's table. Hastings wore a dirty, checked shirt, in addition to sweat-stained Army trousers and troop boots. "Nice horse you got there, mister," he said.

"I like him," Sam replied.

"We want to buy him."

Sam forked another mouthful of *frijoles*. "He

ain't for sale."

Hastings grinned. "Everything's for sale, friend. You just have to know the price."

"I know there ain't no price on that horse."

"Yes, there is," said Hastings. "Your life."

Sam put down his fork. He looked up at Hastings, and his cold blue eyes narrowed even more than usual. He took in the other four deserters. They had passed the bottle again and spread out along the bar, hands resting easily near their pistol butts.

"See, we got to have him," Hastings explained. "Since we got our 'discharges,' we been makin' some bank withdrawals, if you know what I mean. Seems a couple fellas got killed in the process, and now we got posses comin' at us from all directions. If they catch us, it's our necks, so we got to keep one step ahead of them. We can't be ridin' no two men to a horse."

"So walk," Sam told him.

Hastings smiled. "Funny man, eh? Well, I'll tell you what, funny man. Since it's a hot day, and I'm a nice fellow"—the other deserters laughed—"I'll give you another chance. We need that horse. Bein' flush with cash, we was goin' to buy him from you. But now you can just give him to us, as a present. That, or we take him. It's your call."

Martin Cruz's heavy jowls trembled as he pleaded with Sam. "Please, *señor*, give them the *caballo*. I don't want no trouble. When they kill you, I have to dig another grave, and it is so hot today."

Sam gave no answer. Prudently, Martin retreated behind the bar.

Sam eyed the deserters. This was no dime novel. Five against one were odds he wasn't going to beat. Life was a bitch. With a foot, he pushed his chair away from the table. He said, "Take him—if you can."

The five deserters went for their guns. Sam stood, drawing his pistol in the same motion. He cocked it and shot Hastings in the chest. As Hastings went down, Sam crouched and swiveled right to the next man, the one with the forage cap. He fired a fraction of a second before the man fired at him. A hole blossomed in the man's forehead, just under the forage cap's brim. Bullets were flying around Sam. He threw himself to the floor, pointed the pistol upward and fired at a man in a faded blue jacket. He missed and fired again, as bullets gouged the dirt floor near his head. The man in the blue jacket threw up his arms and fell. Lying on the floor, Sam's back was to the last two men. They were only feet away. Even as he cocked the pistol and rolled over, Sam knew his luck had run out.

Two shots sounded from the far corner of the room.

One of the last two deserters spun with a cry. He crashed off the wall and fell. The other man staggered into a table. He fired his pistol into the floor. He tried to raise the pistol again, couldn't, and pitched forward, knocking the table to the floor with him.

Sam looked to the corner. The well-dressed man stood there, with smoking pistols in his hands. The grin on his face made him look younger than he was.

The inside of the cantina was wreathed with acrid black powder smoke. The bodies of the five deserters were sprawled on the floor. Already, flies were buzzing around them. Cruz and his fleshy wife looked up from behind the bar, where they had dived when the shooting had started. The woman saw the carnage and began to wail. Cruz crossed himself and poured a glass of tequila from the bottle that the deserters had left on the bar.

Sam stood. He looked at the stranger. "Don't recall asking for your help," he said.

The man returned his pistols to their holsters. "Let's say I didn't like the odds."

Sam nodded. "I don't enjoy bein' in a man's debt, but I reckon I owe you one."

The well-dressed man picked up his bottle. He got a fresh glass from behind the bar, filled it, and handed it to Sam. "You might want this, now."

Sam did. He drank, feeling the fire slide down his throat, feeling it ease him inside. That had been close. Real close. Sam wondered if there was any paper on the dead men. Probably there hadn't been time for rewards to be offered, if posses were still hot after them. Anyway, he'd gotten this far across the desert on the trail of Thomas Crawford. The nearest Army post was more than a hundred miles off. He wasn't about to go all that way with these dead deserters, then have to start over.

The well-dressed man poured himself a drink. He leaned against the bar, for all the world as if nothing had happened, as if five men had not just died here, as if their bodies were not lying at his feet. Martin Cruz and his wife ventured from behind the bar. They looked at the bodies, then began rifling them, taking the valuables and pocketing them for themselves.

The well-dressed man regarded the Cruzes with amusement. To Sam, he said, "What brings you to this part of the world, friend?"

"Fixin' to cross the *Jornada,*" Sam told him.

The man grinned boyishly. "Not much on the other side, I'm told."

"The Eagle Mountains," Sam said.

"You on a sightseeing trip?"

"Business. I hear there's a band of scalp hunters working out of there. Thought I might join up with them."

"Did you, now? Well, there's a coincidence. I'm off to join the scalp hunters myself."

"Small world," said Sam.

"The Eagle Mountains are big, friend. You have any idea where these scalp hunters might be found?"

"Figured I'd worry about that when I got

there. Why, do you know where they are?"

"As a matter of fact, I do. Since we're both going the same way, what say we travel together?"

Sam Slater hesitated. He was a loner. He didn't like traveling or working with other men, and he was already irritated at being in this fellow's debt.

The well-dressed man went on. "They say the *Jornada*'s a dangerous place. If the Apaches don't get you, thirst will. There's only a few water holes at the best of times, and at this time of year, only a few of those have water in them. You better know where they are if you want to make the journey alive."

"Do you know where they are?" Sam asked.

The well-dressed man spread his hands. "I'm alive, aren't I? Now, what do you say?"

Sam gave in. "All right."

"Good. What's your name?"

"Sam. Sam Simmons."

The boyish-looking fellow held out a hand. "Glad to make your acquaintance, Sam. I'm Ed Fitzpatrick."

Sam shook Fitzpatrick's hand. "When do we leave?"

"When the sun gets lower, and the heat lets up."

"In that case, I'll finish my meal." Sam stepped over the dead men and returned to his table.

By now, Martin Cruz and his wife had taken everything of value from the bodies. They knew there must be money in the saddlebags, and they couldn't wait to get at them. Sometimes trouble had a golden lining. In the meantime, Martin looked up, sweat rolling down his jowls. His voice had a whiny tone. "*Señores*, these bodies. What must I do with them? There are so many. How do I bury them all?"

Sam looked at him. "I'd use a shovel."

CHAPTER 2

THE *JORNADA DEL FUEGO.*

The heat rose in shimmering waves. The sun was suspended overhead like a fiery ball. Nothing moved. Nothing seemed to live in that forbidding wilderness.

Yet there was life. There was saltbush and brittlebush and creosote. There were cholla and prickly pear cactus. There were lizards, snakes, and birds, scorpions and tarantulas. In the few dry washes were mesquite, paloverde, and acacia.

And there were men. Two of them, riding slowly.

Sam Slater and Ed Fitzpatrick had been on the trail since two hours before dawn. Neither man was sweating. Their sweat had long since dried up. The men themselves had dried up. The heat had sucked the moisture from them. It had shriveled them like prunes. And still it beat down, unrelenting, unforgiving, like a living thing, tearing at them. Trying to kill them.

Fitzpatrick wore his expensive shirt open at the neck. Sweat and dirt had turned the collar brown. Even the fierce heat could not blunt his boyish cheerfulness. His white teeth seemed to flash in a perpetual grin. "Why do you want to join the scalp hunters, Sam?"

Sam had known the question was coming. He was prepared for it. "Money," he said. "I'm short, and I hear the Mexes pay good for Apache scalps."

"That the only reason?"

Sam shrugged. "Could be I lost some family to those red bastards."

"Payback, huh?" said Fitzpatrick.

"You can call it that. What about you? You look more like a gambler than a scalp hunter. What brings you to the party?"

Fitzpatrick laughed. "Ah, my friend, like you I am motivated by money. But for me there is also the excitement of the affair, the danger. I guess you could say danger attracts me. I'm addicted to it."

"You talk like you've rode with this bunch before."

"I have," Fitzpatrick said.

"How come you ain't with them now?"

"I've been in Santa Fe, spending my hard-earned money. I have an affinity for the good life, and you can't find that in the Eagle Mountains." He laughed at the thought.

Sam said, "How well do you know Crawford?"

"The colonel? As well as any man can, I suppose—but that's not saying much."

"What's he like?"

Fitzpatrick thought for a moment. "He's a gentleman of some cultivation. Why do you ask?"

"Just wondering. Wondering if he'll take me in."

"I should think he would. Judging from what I saw back at the cantina, you have all the attributes needed to join our band of merry men."

"And what if I didn't?" Sam asked.

Fitzpatrick was cheerful as ever. "Oh, then the colonel would kill you."

Just before noon, they found an outcrop of rock, and they and the horses laid up in its scant shade. Flies buzzed fitfully, as if the heat had stupefied even them; and the horses swished their tails at them without enthusiasm, going through the motions. Sam and Fitzpatrick watered the horses, then themselves. They had brought extra canteens of water as well as oiled canvas bags full of it, but they were still using it at a prodigious rate, mainly because of the horses. Sam gave Fitzpatrick credit. The scalp hunter was no water-wasting greenhorn.

Sam said, "How far is this water hole—what did you call it—Dead Man's Tanks?"

"That's right," Fitzpatrick said. "It's nearer fifteen miles than ten. It'll be a good place to camp the night."

"Sure there's water there?"

"No man can be sure of anything in the *Jornada*, my friend—that's why they call it Dead Man's Tanks. But there was water there when I passed through last month."

Suddenly Sam stood. From out of nowhere, a cold chill rippled up his spine. Deftly, he climbed the rock outcrop, making no noise, the way the Apaches had taught him. Just below the summit, he lay on his stomach and peered at their back trail.

Fitzpatrick climbed behind him, nearly as silent. "What is it?" he asked.

"I don't know," Sam said in a low voice. "A feeling." Carefully, Sam's eyes quartered the ground.

"You think we're being followed?"

"Something like that. You feel it, too?"

Fitzpatrick shook his head. He looked puzzled. "No. You sound like an Indian."

Sam grunted. "I guess I do."

Sam stared for a long time, but he saw nothing. No movement, no dust. The desert looked as vast and empty as ever. At last the two men climbed back down the rocks.

"I guess it was nothing," Sam said. But he couldn't shake the feeling.

Sam and Fitzpatrick waited in the shade until the afternoon was well advanced, then they saddled their mounts and rode out. But Sam kept looking back.

It was within an hour of sundown when they came to the water hole. Dead Man's Tanks lay in the heart of a fortresslike mountain that rose out of the desert. A steep-sided canyon wound its way up into the mountain, and the Tanks lay near the canyon's head. Sam and Fitzpatrick followed the canyon's gravelly bottom, climbing steadily.

"What if there's no water there?" Sam asked.

"Then, my friend, we are in trouble," Fitzpatrick replied.

The Tanks were a *tinaja*, which means "earthen jar" in Spanish. They were eroded cups or holes in a smooth apron of granite, which caught runoff from the desert rains. A large ironwood spread its branches over the Tanks, one of the few signs of life in the canyon. The tree provided shade and prevented the sun from evaporating the water. Grass grew around the edge of the rocks and from cracks in their granite surface. The whickers and restlessness of the horses as they approached told the men that there was water in the Tanks.

The water was scummy brown and thick with old leaves and algae. The edges of the holes were lined with bird droppings and molted feathers. Sam and Fitzpatrick brushed aside the leaves and surface algae, and the dead bugs floating there. While the horses drank, the two men scooped water into their mouths.

The water tasted good.

They camped for the night a ways down the canyon from the water holes. The horses were watered and fed. They were allowed to graze on the little bit of grass around the Tanks, then they were hobbled in a secluded draw. That was Sam's idea. Apaches always hid their horses away from the camp, so an enemy would not be able to find them and run them off in case of attack.

Sam and Fitzpatrick sat by a small fire. Sam had killed a chuckwalla lizard. He skinned it and cooked it. They ate it, along with some tortillas that Fitzpatrick had purchased from Martin Cruz. Sam didn't think that the chuckwalla would agree with Fitzpatrick's cultured palate, but the scalp hunter seemed to enjoy it.

The two men roasted green coffee beans in a skillet that Fitzpatrick provided. They wrapped the roasted beans in their bandanas and crushed them with their pistol butts. Then they mixed the beans with boiling water in their tin cups. They were traveling light—no coffee pot.

As Sam sipped the hot, bitter coffee, Fitzpatrick pulled a bottle of whiskey from his saddlebags. "Here, Sam, try a little of this in there. It's real Kentucky bourbon."

"Thanks," Sam said. He held out his cup, and Fitzpatrick poured in a shot. Sam remembered all the tequila that Fitzpatrick had consumed at the cantina. "You like your snake eye, don't you?"

Fitzpatrick grinned. "Like I said, I have an affinity for the good life."

Suddenly, Sam put down his cup. He stood, slipping his rifle from its saddle scabbard.

"There's somebody out there," he whispered.

Fitzpatrick went for his own rifle. "Apache?"

"White man," Sam said.

"How do you know he's white?"

"I can smell him."

"Smell him? Sam, are you sure you're not part Apache?"

"Sometimes I wonder."

The smell was faint. "He's a ways off, down the canyon," Sam said. "Too far to try a shot at us."

Fitzpatrick said, "That's reassuring, 'cause we make damn good targets by this fire."

"You stay here," Sam told the scalp hunter. "Stay close enough to the fire that he can see you, but not close enough that he can get a good shot."

Fitzpatrick looked faintly amused. "You setting me up as bait?"

"One of us has to do it. I'm going down."

Sam moved quickly and quietly down the canyon. This was the way anyone must come to attack their camp. The canyon's slopes were crowded with boulders. Sam found one and blended in with its darker form. He cocked his rifle and squatted in the sand to wait.

He smelled the man coming closer.

He heard footsteps, climbing the gravelly canyon floor. The footsteps were heavy, cautious.

Sam came to one knee, raising his rifle.

The footsteps went past. Sam could challenge this mysterious visitor, but he doubted that the man came with peaceful intentions. Even if he had, it was his tough luck for being so stupid about it.

Sam fired.

There was an oath. Then an orange flame split the darkness, along with a rifle shot.

Sam fired at the flash. He rolled to one side as an answering shot whined off the rock next to where he had been standing. Sam's rifle blasted into the night, twice. He heard footsteps hobbling away in the darkness.

Sam waited. It was pointless to follow the man now. He could walk into the same kind of trap he himself had just set. As he waited, he absently rubbed the scar that ran from his left sideburn to the corner of his mouth. Whenever he touched the scar, he remembered the way his cheek had flapped open when his uncle had sliced it with the knife. He remembered how that had felt. He had only been fifteen at the time, and it had scared the hell out of him. It still did.

He remained where he was until dawn. It was his Apache training. He could remain an entire day in one spot, motionless, under the worst conditions. Whoever this visitor had been, he was gone. As the flat gray light spread into the canyon, Sam looked for the man's tracks.

He found them. The man had been big. Real

big. Sam found something else. Blood.

There was a noise, and Sam turned, to see Fitzpatrick making his way down the canyon, rifle in hand.

"Well, that was an interesting night," Fitzpatrick commented dryly. "Did you get him?"

"Winged him." Sam pointed to the bloodstains. "From the looks of this blood, it wasn't enough to finish him." He peered back down the lightening canyon. There was no sign of the man. "I wonder what he wanted?"

"He wanted me," Fitzpatrick said.

"You? Why?"

"I'm a scalp hunter, Sam, there's a bounty on my head. Five hundred dollars. He could probably collect on you now, too, come to think of it. That cantina owner, Cruz, must have heard us talking. He must have put the fellow on to us."

"Comin' out into the *Jornada*—that's a hell of a risk to take for a thousand dollars."

Fitzpatrick shrugged. "Some men like that kind of work. Some men don't know any other kind. They have to take the risks as they come."

Sam shifted uneasily. Fitzpatrick could have been talking about him. Sam wondered what would happen if the time came for him to kill Fitzpatrick. He was starting to like the boyish scalp hunter. He wondered what he would have to do to get Crawford. He'd be outnumbered up in the Eagles—likely twenty or twenty-five to one. He wasn't going in with a plan. He figured he'd let things develop. Then again, that was part of the challenge, and challenge was what he liked.

"We got three choices," Sam explained. "We can go after this fellow. We can stay here by the water, wait for him to get thirsty and come to us. Or we can continue on."

Fitzpatrick said, "Let's go on. That clown is probably halfway back to Cruz's cantina by now. I think you ran him off."

"I hope so," Sam said. "Come on. We should have been on the trail hours ago."

CHAPTER 3

SAM AND FITZPATRICK RODE ON.

There was no sense in trying to make up the time they had lost. Time stood still in the *Jornada.* Sam suspected that Fitzpatrick suffered from a hangover. The scalp hunter must have helped himself to that whiskey last night, while Sam had been waiting for the return of their mysterious visitor. Alcohol could dehydrate a man, though, and dehydration was a dangerous thing in this country.

They were in the heart of the passage. It was rugged, rocky country, broken only by an occasional clump of creosote. The trail was marked by the remains of those who had gone before.

There were discarded articles of clothing, saddles dry-rotted in the sun, with their stitching burst open. There was a wagon, its once gay paint faded and chipped. There were warped pieces of furniture, someone's prized possessions, abandoned because they'd been too heavy to carry further. There were boxes of old books, photographs, and other personal effects. There was even a piano. People's hopes and dreams, come to nothing in this sun-scorched hell.

There were the bones of animals—horses, mules, oxen, a dog—long since picked clean by scavengers.

"Buzzards seem to make a good living in these parts," Sam commented.

Fitzpatrick nodded. "They stay fat, all right. They're the only ones that do."

There were graves, too—men, women, children. Who had these people been, Sam wondered. Settlers, prospectors, soldiers, outlaws on the run. Dreamers, looking for new lives, only to come to grief under the unforgiving sun. Most had died of thirst, some probably of hunger. Sam and Fitzpatrick found human bones beside the trail, as well, and they bore evidence of different ends. One skull had a small hole neatly drilled in the front, and a larger hole in the back where the bullet had come out. Another skull had been caved in, cracked like an eggshell, by a heavy object wielded with unimaginable ferocity.

"Apaches," remarked Fitzpatrick. "They sort

of enforce the vagrancy laws around here. They keep the buzzards fed."

Sam removed his hat and ran a hand through his dirty blond hair. "I don't know who picked your hide-out, but you got one hell of a barrier between you and the law."

"The colonel picked it," Fitzpatrick said. "And you're right. We're protected by the *Jornada* on one side, the mountains and the Mexican border on the other. We're damn near untouchable. That's what's kept us in business so long. You'd need a large party to wipe us out, and a large party would never get across the *Jornada.* There's not enough water. The Army's tried to get us once or twice, but they gave up, too. Besides, they got their hands full chasing Apaches."

"How long you been with the scalp hunters, anyway?" Sam asked.

Fitzpatrick laughed. "Long enough, my friend. Long enough. Sometimes it seems like forever."

Noon came. There was no shade. Sam and Fitzpatrick unsaddled their horses and sat in the animals' shadows. After dozing a couple of hours in the ferocious heat, they rose.

"The next water's at a seep spring in the foothills," Fitzpatrick said. "We won't reach it until sometime tomorrow."

"How do you know where these water holes are?" Sam asked him.

Fitzpatrick shrugged matter-of-factly.

"Apaches told us—before they died."

Sam tapped the oiled canvas water bags hanging from their saddles. "We're already running low," he said.

The two men filled their hats and gave the water to the horses, saving just a swallow for themselves.

"We won't get any less thirsty standing around here," Sam said. "Let's go."

They started off, walking the horses for a while, taking it easy on them. Both men wore knee-high Apache moccasins. Fitzpatrick had lost some of his cheerful disposition. He was having trouble from drinking so much the night before. But he was tough. He didn't complain. At one point, though, he swooned, stumbled, and sat heavily.

Sam knelt beside him. "I ought to leave you here, for being so stupid," he told Fitzpatrick.

Fitzpatrick grinned at him. "Do that, and you'll never find Colonel Crawford's camp."

Sam swore to himself. He took Fitzpatrick's canteen. "This got whiskey in it, or water?"

"Water," Fitzpatrick assured him.

"I'm surprised," Sam said. He gave the scalp hunter a good long drink of their precious liquid.

The water revived Fitzpatrick. He smiled at Sam through a screaming headache. "Thanks," he said.

"Yeah," said Sam. He helped the scalp

hunter to his feet. Fitzpatrick winced with pain, and the two men continued on.

That night, they made a cold camp. There was no wood for a fire, and, anyway, neither man liked the idea of a fire way out here in the open. They sat beneath the stars. From his saddlebags, Fitzpatrick brought out a fresh bottle of whiskey.

Sam couldn't believe it. "You got to be crazy. Didn't you learn your lesson today?"

Fitzpatrick had recovered some of his spirit. He grinned at Sam. "I can't get to sleep without it."

Sam shook his head.

Fitzpatrick took a drink from the bottle. "That's a hell of a scar you've got, Sam. How'd you come by it?"

"Fella sliced me," Sam said noncommittally.

"He have a reason?"

Sam gave the scalp hunter a look. "He was trying to force his 'attentions' on a girl."

"And you stopped him?"

"Stopped him dead," Sam said.

Fitzpatrick took another drink. "Bad *hombre*?"

"When he was drinking, he was. He was my uncle. She was his daughter."

Fitzpatrick thought about that. "Seems like you did a good thing." He held out the bottle. "Sure you don't want some?"

"No thanks," Sam said.

Late the next morning, the two men turned off the trail and entered the rugged hills.

Fitzpatrick said that the seep spring was in a box canyon. They made their way up a rocky ledge that led to the canyon's entrance. The horses picked their way with care. Suddenly, from beneath a nearby overhang, came the warning buzz of a rattlesnake.

Sam's horse reared. That movement saved Sam's life, because just as the animal moved, a bullet hummed by Sam's head, followed by the flat report of a rifle shot.

Sam struggled to control the horse. There was another shot; Sam didn't hear the bullet. Drawing his rifle, he threw himself from the saddle and scrambled for cover farther down the overhang. He hoped there wasn't a den of snakes in there. He heard the clatter of hoofs, as Fitzpatrick dropped over the ledge and down into a protected trough.

Sam stuck his head up, risking a look. A shot made him duck back down. The shot had come from above them. The weapon sounded like a high-powered hunting rifle.

"See him?" called Fitzpatrick.

"Not yet," Sam answered.

He looked again. Another shot whined off the rock near him, the chips cutting his cheek. He ducked again. He dabbed at his bleeding cheek with a dirty hand.

"That was too close for comfort," he muttered.

"I saw the smoke," said Fitzpatrick. "He's in that jumble of boulders just above us."

Sam nodded.

"Could be an Apache, trying to lure us into an ambush," Fitzpatrick went on.

"Could be," Sam said. "Could be our friend from the other night. Hell, in this country, it could be just about anybody."

Fitzpatrick said, "We can't stay here. We'll fry up like a couple of Texas steaks."

Sam agreed. "Let's flush him out."

"I'll go first," said Fitzpatrick. "You ready?"

"Yeah."

"All right—now!"

Sam snapped a shot toward the boulders. As he did, Fitzpatrick broke from cover. He raced upward and to his left. He threw himself behind some rocks and lay there, catching his breath and waiting for the throbbing in his head to subside. Then he got to one knee and motioned for Sam to be ready. He reared up and fired toward the boulders.

As he did, Sam broke right. He heard another shot and felt something part the air near him. He dove to the ground near the next cover, a small pile of rocks, and wriggled forward on his belly.

Fitzpatrick's turn again. Sam covered him. Then it was Sam's turn. Then they repeated the procedure, moving in a widening semicircle, aiming to come in behind the boulders and to catch their adversary between them. Fitzpatrick was almost level with the man's position, now.

The unknown rifleman fired at the scalp hunter as he dashed forward. Sam saw the smoke, and he smiled grimly to himself.

Got you, he thought.

Sam got ready to move.

Suddenly there came the sound of hoofs. Sam and Fitzpatrick both ran forward, as a horse and rider broke from cover. Sam had a glimpse of a huge man with a long blond pigtail. The man was built like a beer barrel with a head. There was a bandage on his left shoulder. Sam and Fitzpatrick snapped shots at the man and missed, then horse and rider disappeared behind a rocky hill.

Sam and Fitzpatrick ran together. They heard the horse, but the man was lost to sight behind the hill. They waited for him to come into the open again, below them.

"He's big, and he's wounded," Sam said. "It's got to be our friend from the other night."

A minute later, man and horse broke cover. The man galloped away, using his mount recklessly on the treacherous, broken ground. A plume of dust rose behind him.

With a smile, Sam raised his rifle. He aimed, held his breath, and squeezed the trigger.

The distant horse reared and fell, throwing its huge rider. The pigtailed man hit hard, then scrambled for cover, as the animal thrashed in its death throes.

Sam swore. He hadn't been aiming at the

horse. "You ever see that fella before?" he asked Fitzpatrick.

The scalp hunter shook his head. "If I have, I don't remember it. You going to go after him?"

"No. Without a horse, he's no threat to us now. Go after him, and we'd use up time and water—and we might get ourselves shot into the bargain. If he can get himself out of this, good luck to him."

"How did he manage to get ahead of us, anyhow?"

Sam had thought about that. "He didn't run away the other night. While we sat and waited for him to come back, he mounted up and headed south. He had this place picked out for an ambush. He took a parallel trail, so we wouldn't pick up his tracks."

"He must know the *Jornada,*" Fitzpatrick said.

Sam nodded grimly. "He's fixin' to know it a whole lot better."

Fitzpatrick grinned. "I thought the buzzards looked a mite peckish."

They got their horses and continued on, leaving their attacker, whoever he was, to his fate. Sam had an uneasy feeling that, despite what Fitzpatrick had said, the unknown rifleman had not been after scalp hunters. He had a feeling that the man's bullets had been meant for him alone. But why? Sam did not know.

It was well past midafternoon when they neared the entrance to the box canyon. Both men's lips were swollen and cracked. Sam began taking wide swings to the left and right.

"What is it?" said Fitzpatrick.

"Looking for sign. I want to see if anybody's been here before us."

One of the first things Sam had learned from the Apaches was never to go straight into any situation. An Apache would check it from every conceivable angle before committing himself.

They reached the box canyon. Fitzpatrick started in.

"Wait," said Sam.

Fitzpatrick turned.

"Is there another way in?"

"One," Fitzpatrick said. "But it would be hard for horses."

"Let's look at it before we go to the spring."

"Sam, there's no one here, and we're dying of thirst. These animals . . ."

"It's dying of other causes that worries me," Sam said.

"You got that feeling again?"

"Yep."

The scalp hunter sighed. "I can't argue with you, then."

They rode into the hills, around the canyon. They hid the horses in an arroyo and went on by foot, carrying their rifles. They worked their way just below the ridge line, so they'd have a good view of the surroundings, but wouldn't be sky-lighted.

Sam led the way. Fitzpatrick followed, wincing because the climb affected his sore head. "You sure this is necessary?" he said.

Sam didn't answer. He moved carefully, quietly, never taking a step till he'd scouted it out.

"How far?" he whispered to Fitzpatrick.

"We should be right above it."

Sam moved downward, following an old animal track. Suddenly he put up a hand. Behind him, Fitzpatrick stopped.

Sam moved behind some rocks, then waved Fitzpatrick forward. From their hiding place, the two men looked down.

Below, they saw the seep spring. Around the spring was an oasis of tall cottonwoods and sycamores. There were yellow monkey flowers and bluebells. There was lush deer grass and clover.

There were also men at the spring, getting water.

The men were Apaches.

CHAPTER 4

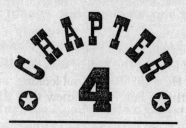

THERE WERE SIX OF THE APACHES. THEY were painted for war, and they were armed with the latest model rifles and pistols. Hobbled horses grazed around the seep spring. There were more horses than Indians. The Apaches drank alertly, their eyes moving, like wolves.

"Netdahe," Sam said in a low voice. "I recognize their paint."

"I know them," said Fitzpatrick. "They're considered renegades, even by the other Apaches."

Sam nodded. "They're recruited from other bands, some of 'em. There's Navajos and Mexicans among 'em, too. This bunch is returning from a raid, that's why they've got all the horses. We're damn lucky they didn't hear the shooting, earlier."

Sam's ice-blue eyes were constantly moving, like those of the Indians. Then they stopped, as saw the war party's leader. The Indian was old, seventy if he was a day. He was tall and frail looking, and walked with an arthritic limp. Sam knew that the Indian's looks belied his true nature, however.

Sam said, "See that old one? That's the leader. That's Nanay."

"Nanay!" said Fitzpatrick in surprise. "I heard Nanay was dead."

"He looks lively enough to me."

"How can you be sure it's him?"

"I know him," Sam said. "I've met him."

"Your knowledge of Apaches is considerable."

Sam did not tell Fitzpatrick that he had lived with the Apaches, that he'd been partially raised by them. He'd already told Fitzpatrick more than he wanted to about himself. He did not want to give any more clues that might, in Fitzpatrick's mind, link Sam Simmons to Sam Slater, the notorious Regulator. "I used to scout for the government," he explained.

"They say Nanay's as bad as they come," Fitzpatrick said.

"He is," Sam replied. "But he wasn't always that way. He's a Chihenne, originally, a Warm Springs Apache. They're the most peaceable band—or they were. Nanay actually liked white men, until we kicked him and his people off the reservation where we had told them they could live forever. Seems some damn fool was afraid there might be a few nuggets of gold or silver up there, and civilization would come to an end if the white people weren't allowed to find it. After that, Nanay and Victorio went on the warpath. When Victorio was killed, Nanay joined the Netdahe."

Fitzpatrick's eyes had come alight. "The governor of Sonora had a standing reward of five thousand pesos for Nanay's scalp. Well, actually, for Nanay, it would have to be his head. If we could trap his band . . ."

"They live in Mexico," Sam pointed out.

"That's no problem. We've been to Mexico before. Apaches in the States are just about fished out, anyway, unless you go onto the reservations." He laughed quietly. "Not that we haven't done that a time or two."

Sam restrained himself. He had to remember what he was supposed to be. He said, "I hope you don't run out of 'em too soon. I ain't made any money off 'em, yet."

Fitzpatrick grinned. "I like you, Sam. You're direct. I admire that in a man."

Sam said nothing. He wondered if Fitzpatrick would think so much of him when he found out who he really was, and why he was here.

During all this time, Sam had alternated between watching the Apaches and the rocky heights surrounding the box canyon.

"You spotted their lookouts?" Fitzpatrick asked him.

Sam nodded. "There's two. They're watching the two entrances to the canyon. They weren't expecting anybody to come across the top. Still, we're lucky they didn't see us." With a thumb, he tilted his hat back. "All in all, I'd say that this has been our lucky day."

Fitzpatrick said, "Think this bunch will camp here?"

"I would," Sam said.

"What do we do, then?"

"Stay put. If we move, there's too much chance of them seeing us. We've pushed our luck about as much as I care to. Anyway, we've got to have that water."

"And our horses?"

"We can't go back for them. We have to hope they don't smell the water and give themselves away."

"In other words, we wait," said Fitzpatrick.

"Yep. We wait."

The Apaches camped at the seep spring. They led all but one of their horses away, to be hidden. They built a fire. Then they killed and roasted the remaining horse, after eating the best cuts, like the liver and part of the intestines, raw. The two white men heard them talking and laughing. The lookouts came in from the hills, to be replaced by two more.

All this time Sam and Fitzpatrick lay in the

rocks, sucking pebbles, trying to ignore their thirst. Sam was glad they hadn't brought a pack mule. The damn thing would have raised so much racket, the Apaches would have heard them miles away. They'd have searched the hills until they found the mule's owners. Sam hoped the horses would not be found by the Indians or attacked by coyotes. He did not want to be left on foot in this country, like that pigtailed man who'd been tailing them.

The sun set in a blaze of purple and gold. Twilight descended on the box canyon. In the rocks, a chill wind picked up. Fitzpatrick, who liked his creature comforts, remarked, "That fire looks inviting."

Sam snorted. "They'd be just as happy roasting us over it as that horse." He was glad the wind was blowing away from the spring, so the Apaches would not smell him or his companion.

Soon, it was dark. "We'll take turns on guard," Sam said, fingering his rifle.

"All right," said Fitzpatrick.

"I'll go first." Sam looked over. "Can you get to sleep without your bottle?"

"It'll be hard," Fitzpatrick admitted. Then he grinned. "Though I don't know how much sleep I want to get with Nanay and his friends around."

"You always drink yourself out?"

"Most nights, I do. It started during the war. Some of the things I saw . . . some of the things I did. It was the only way I could deal with them. Plus, you're so keyed up in battle, so excited. Alcohol is a way to relax. Haven't you ever felt like that?"

"Not on a regular basis," Sam admitted. "There a lot of war veterans among the scalp hunters?"

"Some," said Fitzpatrick. "We're like the Netdahe—renegades. We've got a little bit of everything."

"Did you know Colonel Crawford in the war?"

"What? No. I mean, I could hardly be expected to. It was a big war."

Sam and Fitzpatrick stayed in the rocks all night. Neither man slept much. They were too thirsty, and too scared.

The Apaches awoke well before dawn. While some built up the fire, others scouted the area thoroughly and brought in the horses. Sam and Fitzpatrick held their breaths as one of the scouts came near them. But the Apache—a boy, a novice warrior—missed them in the dim light. When the scouts returned, the Apaches ate some more of the horse meat. They filled their water bags, which were the intestines of horses and cattle, and they tied off the ends with rawhide. Slinging the bags over their shoulders, they departed. They went out the way they had come in, driving their captured horses over the more difficult northern pass.

"We'll wait before we go down," Sam said. "They'll be watching their back trail."

Fitzpatrick hugged himself against the dawn chill. "The plan has changed, Sam. We're going to follow Nanay."

Sam looked at him dubiously.

"We're scalp hunters, Sam. Those Apaches are money in the bank. A lot of money. Colonel Crawford will want to hear about this. He'll want to know which direction they were headed, so he can get an idea where their camp is. After that, Perico can take over."

"Who's Perico?" asked Sam.

"Our tame Apache—if there's such a thing as a tame Apache. He finds them for us."

"He betrays his own people?"

Fitzpatrick shrugged. "He does it for the excitement, like me. Plus, the money keeps him in whiskey. He's no different than the Apaches who scout for the Army—except we pay him better."

Sam looked away. He was worried that this Perico might know him. Sam didn't recognize Perico's name, but that didn't mean much. Apaches, like most Indians, could change their names.

The hot sun made its appearance. Sam and Fitzpatrick waited, but the Apaches did not return. At last, the two men stood, stiffly. They worked the kinks out of their bodies, then moved down to the spring where they knelt and drank.

Fitzpatrick stretched full length on the ground, scooping the cold water with both hands. Unlike the water at the Tanks, this water was sweet and fresh, forced out of underground streams by pressures deep within the earth. "God, that's good," Fitzpatrick said. Sam drank sparingly, watching the surrounding rocks, alert for trouble.

They went back for the horses and brought

the animals to the spring. They watered them, fed them, then set them out to graze. After going so long without water, the beasts were in no shape for travel yet.

Sam and Fitzpatrick filled their canteens and water bags. They munched jerky and corn dodgers. It was past midday when they started on the trail of the Apaches.

"I don't want to get too close to them," Fitzpatrick said. "The last thing we need is to bump into the rear of an Apache war party."

The Indians' tracks were easy to follow for Sam, because of the shod horses they had stolen on their raid.

Fitzpatrick said, "What'll they do with all these horses—the ones they don't eat, that is?"

"Sell 'em to the Mexicans for *aguardiente* and ammunition," Sam said. "When they ain't raiding the Mexicans, they trade with 'em. It's an interesting relationship. They don't want to wipe the Mexicans out, 'cause then there'd be nothing for them to steal. They look on the Mexicans as a sort of farm, to be harvested from time to time."

Soon the Apache trail broke up. "They'll scatter, then meet this evening at a prearranged spot," Sam said.

They followed two sets of the shod hoofs. The next day, they reached the *tinaja* where the Apaches had camped. They rested a while and continued on.

The trail followed a steady southeast course.

There were no twists, no turns, none of the tricks Apaches usually played. Sam said, "Wherever they got these horses, they must not have left any survivors. By the time the army figures out there's even been a raid, Nanay will be back in Mexico."

"The Sierra Negros," Fitzpatrick decided at the next halt. "That's where their camp must be. The trail leads straight there. I don't think we need go any farther. We'll let Perico do the rest."

They turned in a southwesterly direction, back toward the Eagle Mountains. Fitzpatrick looked sheepish. "I'm afraid I don't know this part of the *Jornada*. I don't know where the water is."

That evening, they camped in a dry wash. Sam found a young paloverde, and they dug near it until they reached water.

The next day, they continued on. They cut off the tops of barrel cactus and sucked water from the cactus meat with a cane Apache drinking reed that Sam carried. They dug out more of the meat and squeezed water from it into their hats, for the horses.

At the end of that day, they left the *Jornada del Fuego*. They were in the Eagle Mountains.

Fitzpatrick led the way. The mountains were wild and rugged. The cactus and mesquite at the lower levels gave way to oaks and sycamores, then to cool pines and cedars. The going was hard. Sam was glad he'd come with Fitzpatrick, now. He could have wandered in this maze of blind canyons for years before finding the scalp hunters.

At last, Fitzpatrick brought them out of the high mountains into a wide, level valley, with a pleasant stream flowing through it. Across the valley, a promontory stuck out of the hills, a natural fortress. On the promontory were the ruins of a Spanish mission.

Sam and Fitzpatrick rode across the valley. A well-used trail brought them into the hills, then across a narrow rock ledge, like a causeway, that led to the promontory and the mission. A stone wall guarded the entrance to the promontory.

The two men had been seen as soon as they entered the valley, and a crowd of men and women waited for them on the causeway and at the wall's carved wooden gates. The men wore all manner of dress—buckskins, Mexican sombreros, plug hats, cowboy garb. Even here in camp, they went heavily armed. The women were Mexican and, for the most part, slatternly. All seemed happy to see the newcomers. Many of them waved.

"Welcome back, Colonel," they cried.

Sam looked at his companion. An icy finger seemed to touch Sam's heart. "Colonel?" he said.

Fitzpatrick grinned boyishly. "Yes. Forgive me, Sam, but my real name isn't Fitzpatrick. It's Crawford. Thomas Crawford."

CHAPTER 5

SAM STARED.

"Why didn't you tell me?" he said.

Crawford's grin broadened, and he laughed. "How did I know I could trust you? There's five *thousand* dollars on my head, not five hundred. That's a powerful temptation to any man. Who knows, you might have been a bounty hunter yourself."

Sam could have kicked himself. Fate had thrown Crawford right into his lap, and he had missed his chance. It would have been so easy.

And now . . .

Now Sam didn't know what he'd do. Oh, well, he was no worse off than he'd expected to be at this point.

He forced himself to grin at Crawford. "I guess you put one over on me."

Crawford laughed again and turned to the crowd. "Boys, this is my friend, Sam Simmons. He's going to be riding with us."

Before he could say any more, a woman's voice rang out. "Thomas!"

A pretty, dark-haired girl pushed her way through the crowd and ran up to Crawford with open arms. Crawford lifted her up into the saddle with him, and they embraced. The girl looked part Mexican and part Indian. She wore tiers of jangling bracelets and necklaces. The smell of perfume wafted from her.

Crawford kissed her again, then held her at arm's length. "Teresa, how have you been?"

"Better, now that you are here," she pouted.

"Miss me?"

"You know I did."

Crawford—it was hard to think of him as Crawford, and not Fitzpatrick—kissed her a third time. "Wait till you see what I brought you from Santa Fe," he said. Then he turned. "Come on, Sam."

The two men and the woman rode through the mission gates. They halted in front of the church. The church was about a hundred and fifty years old, Sam guessed. It, and the buildings surrounding it, had fallen into a state of considerable disrepair.

Crawford handed the girl down, then he dismounted, along with Sam. A Mexican came up to take their horses. Crawford put an arm around the girl's shoulder. "Teresa, this is Sam."

The girl's dark eyes met Sam's. "Hello, Sam."

Sam touched his hat brim. "Ma'am."

"Make yourself at home, Sam," Crawford said expansively. "Teresa and I have some "—he winked—"old times to catch up on. Pitch your gear anywhere; we're informal here. You and I will talk later."

Crawford started to lead the girl away, when his path was blocked by a wiry fellow, who stood with his head cocked to one side. "Nice to see you back, Colonel."

Arm in arm with Teresa, Crawford grinned at the man. "Why, thanks, Quirt."

The man called Quirt had a long jaw, high cheekbones, and small eyes. His flat-brimmed hat was tilted well back on his head, revealing prematurely gray hair. He wore leather wrist guards, and a plaited rawhide quirt dangled from his right hand. Part of the little finger on his left hand was missing. He spoke with a deep, flat voice. "Some of the boys been getting restless."

"I've been getting a little restless myself," Crawford admitted.

"Yeah, but you been in Santa Fe, living it up. We been stuck here."

"Nobody said you had to stay," Crawford told him.

"Any idea when we might be riding again?"

"As a matter of fact, I have. Does the name Nanay mean anything to you?"

"Nanay?" said Quirt, puzzled. "Nanay's dead. The *rurales* killed him last year near Ures."

"No, the Mexicans didn't get him."

Quirt frowned. "How do you know?"

"Because I saw him, two days ago, in the *Jornada.*"

"What makes you think it was Nanay you saw?"

Crawford glanced toward Sam. "Mr. Simmons, here, is a personal acquaintance of Nanay's. He recognized him."

Quirt shifted his gaze to Sam. "Did he, now? Where'd you find this bird, anyway?"

"On the edge of the *Jornada.* I helped him shoot some stray dogs."

"Why should he be one of us?" Quirt complained. "Scalp bounties ain't been all that good lately, and we got us enough ways to split the money as it is."

Crawford's usually jovial mood grew serious. "He's one of us because I say he is. You got a problem with that?"

"I don't like his look," Quirt said. "I don't trust him."

"It's what I like that counts around here, Quirt. Don't forget that."

The air became suddenly tense. Quirt didn't push it, though. Chastened, he said nothing.

Smiling again, Crawford said, "Sam will be an asset to our group, I assure you. He's quite a hand with firearms. He also knows the Apaches. Think about Nanay. That's a possible five thousand pesos in our pockets that we wouldn't have, except for Sam. If it hadn't been for Sam recognizing Nanay, we'd probably be getting ready to do another reservation job. Come to think of it, if it hadn't been for Sam, I'd probably still be roasting over a fire at the seep spring."

He turned to Sam. "Sam, this is Quirt Evans. He's been with us from the start."

The two men did not shake hands. Sam eyed Quirt. "Easy to see how you got your handle."

Evans held up his quirt and looked at it admiringly. "You don't know the half of it. See this? I killed a man with this, up in the Nations. Flayed him alive."

"Gee," said Sam, "you're real tough, ain't you?"

Quirt bristled. "Maybe someday you'll get a chance to find out how tough I am."

"I'm scared," Sam said.

"All right, you two," Crawford told them. "That's enough." He raised his voice. "Where's Perico?"

A lithe, medium-sized Apache stepped from the crowd. The Apache had a handsome, almost girlish face. He wore a breechclout and a purple calico shirt. A knife and revolver were belted around his waist. Sam breathed a sigh of relief. He didn't know Perico. He could tell from Perico's headband and moccasins that he was a Warm Springs Apache, like Nanay had been.

"*Sí, mi coronel?*" said the Apache.

Crawford told Perico about Nanay. The Apache's impassive face grew animated when he heard the name of his old chief. Crawford told him how the raiding party's tracks had run toward the Sierra Negros. "Take some horses and food. See if you can find their camp."

"*Sí, mi coronel,*" said Perico. He turned and started for the stables.

Crawford turned back to Sam. "And now, my friend, if you'll excuse us?"

Crawford led Teresa toward one of the mission outbuildings. As the crowd broke up, one of the scalp hunters shouted, "Fandango tonight, Colonel?"

"Damn right," Crawford told them.

The men whooped.

Meanwhile, Sam set out to explore his new surroundings.

CHAPTER 6

SAM WALKED AROUND THE PROMONTORY and mission grounds. It was easy to see why the mission had been established here, instead of in the valley. There was a well in front of the church, built over an underground spring; and on three sides, the drop was steep, almost unclimbable.

Sam smiled. Apaches prided themselves on their ability to climb. Folks went on about getting up that mountain in Europe, the Matterhorn. If they wanted it climbed, all they had to do was send a few Apaches. In reality, this mission was little safer than it would have been in the valley. Still, it had probably given the Franciscan missionaries and their Pima flocks a sense of security.

Down below, along the stream, was an ill-tended cornfield. Here and there were cattle, several of which were being led up to the promontory, to be slaughtered for the fandango.

The mission church's white dome glowed golden in the late afternoon sun. The church was long and narrow, with a columned and decorated facade. Most of the roof was gone, and the plaster had come off what was left of the walls, revealing the fieldstone underneath. Next to the church was the bell tower. The hundred-pound brass bell was still in place beneath the cupola at the top, still ready to ring the faithful to prayer.

On the church's eastern side was a cloister for the monks. Its wooden columns were in decay; its grounds were overgrown with weeds. There had been an adobe wall around the church, but its bricks had crumbled with time or had been removed to build houses for the Pimas, who had stayed on the promontory after the mission itself had been abandoned. There were numerous outbuildings—kitchen, stables, store sheds—all in ruins.

A century and a half earlier, this promontory had been the site of a flourishing community. Now, it was home only to ghosts—and to the scalp hunters. The scalp hunters were a tough bunch. They had to be, if their job was taking human hair. Their women were just as tough. Some of the scalp hunters lived in the abandoned buildings. Others had built crude *jacales* around the promontory. There was even a cantina.

The old Franciscans would have been shocked at that. They would have been shocked at the filth, as well. The main form of garbage disposal seemed to consist of throwing it off the cliff. Scrawny chickens ran here and there. A goat bawled.

Sam went inside the church. The old cross over the entrance tilted crazily. Narrow windows added light to that provided by the missing roof. Faded frescoes depicting the life of Christ—painted by the Indians—decorated the walls. Some of the scalp hunters were living here. The place reeked of unwashed bodies. A few men had curtained off spaces for themselves. From behind one set of curtains came a woman's giggle.

Sam went to the corral and got his saddle and gear. He pitched them against an open spot along the walls of what had once been the sacristy. Then he left the church. Bands of mauve, gold, and crimson streaked the evening sky. The long shadows were softening.

"There you are," said a voice. It was Crawford.

Sam turned. The scalp hunter came up, flashing his boyish grin. He had been drinking; Sam could smell the liquor on his breath.

"Settling in all right?" Crawford asked.

Sam nodded.

"Sorry about that trick I played on you."

So am I, Sam thought. "That's all right," he said. "I don't blame you."

"What do you think of our little setup here? Impressive, isn't it."

"Yeah. How long you been here?"

"A little more than a year. We used to camp in the mountains, about forty miles from here, but the Apaches found us there. They almost got us. They'd give anything to eliminate us."

Sam and Crawford walked across the mission grounds. Behind them, the two steers were being slaughtered for the fandango. Other men readied a bonfire.

"How'd you get into this business, anyway?" asked Sam.

Crawford shrugged. "Like I told you before, for the excitement, the adventure. After the war, I couldn't let go. I had to have the same kind of stimulation."

"Why didn't you stay in the Army?"

"I did. Of course, they only let me stay on as a lieutenant. I didn't like that, but I could accept it. I was lucky to even get a commission, with no West Point background. Then I got into an argument with another officer, over a woman. I'd been drinking, and there was a fight. I shot the fellow. He didn't die, but I was forced to resign my commission."

"They call you colonel. Was that your rank in the war?"

Crawford nodded. "I commanded my own regiment at the end. Those were some times, I'll tell you."

"You were young for that much rank."

Crawford snorted. "Age means nothing, my friend. Custer was a general at twenty-three, and he was the biggest idiot that ever put on a uniform."

"What did you do before the war?"

"I read law. Hadn't been for the war, I'd probably have been a small-town attorney, like my father. But when the fight started, I joined up. I rose through the ranks, and things were never the same after that. I couldn't go back to the life I'd known before."

"And after you resigned?" Sam said.

"I drifted. I wanted to go to Mexico and fight for the French, but that war ended before I could get there. So, I did some scouting for the Army. I hunted buffalo—that was an awful job. I was even a cow-town peace officer for a while. Then I heard about this Mexican bounty on scalps. That appealed to me. I recruited some men, and the rest, as they say, is history. What about you, where are you from?"

"No place in particular," Sam said.

"What trade have you followed?"

"This and that."

"Not very forthcoming, are you?"

"Not very," Sam admitted.

"You sound like a man with a price on his head."

"That's possible."

Crawford laughed. Just then, Teresa came over to them. She smoothed her sleek hair, which was rumpled from what she and Crawford had been doing, and adjusted her low-cut blouse. She took Crawford's arm, and as she did, her dark eyes met Sam's for the second time that day.

Sam returned the gaze.

"The dancing will start soon," she told Crawford.

"All right," said Crawford. He turned to Sam. "Come join the fun."

Sam wondered how he could kill this man, get the body out, then escape with it across the *Jornada.* He'd like to kill all the scalp hunters—they would bring a tidy sum—but there were too many.

"All right," he told Crawford. *I'll have my fun later,* he thought.

Fandango.

The scalp hunters had built a bonfire in front of the old mission church. Crackling logs showered sparks into the night sky. Guitarists and fiddlers played. There was dancing and hollering. Men danced with women and with other men, the designated "woman" wearing a kerchief tied around his sleeve. The slaughtered steers turned on spits. There were tubs of home-brewed beer and kegs of mescal that the scalp hunters had purchased in villages over the border. They didn't have much contact with the States, because of the *Jornada,* and because most were wanted men. There was probably paper on three-quarters of them, Sam figured, and not just for the crime of scalp hunting. It was a golden harvest, and Sam couldn't reap it.

Crawford and Teresa danced with the rest. Crawford's boyish face was flushed with liquor. Teresa's low-cut blouse flounced provocatively.

They stopped in front of Sam. "Come on, Sam," said Crawford. "Find yourself a partner."

Sam smiled thinly. "I ain't much of a dancer."

Teresa took a step forward. "I'll dance with you." She held out a bejeweled hand. "Come on, I won't hurt you."

For a moment, Crawford looked askance. Then he said, "It's all right, Sam."

"No thanks," Sam said at last. "I think I'll sit this one out. Don't want to break nobody's toes."

Teresa shrugged. She and Crawford began dancing again.

Sam strolled to the adobe cantina on the far edge of the promontory. An enterprising Mexican had realized the business the scalp hunters could bring, and he'd built this place for them.

Sam went in. The inside was crude, lit with candles.The owner languished behind his plank bar. In one corner, Quirt Evans and three other men played cards. Everyone else was at the fandango.

"*Aguardiente*," Sam told the owner.

"*Sí*." The Mexican, sweaty and covered with boils, poured the clear liquid into a dirty glass. Sam tasted it and made a face.

The card players spotted Sam. "Hey, Simmons," said a greasy-faced one named Slocum. "Care to sit in?"

Sam made a gesture of futility with his hand.

"No money."

One of the other scalp hunters raised scraggly eyebrows in disbelief. "You mean to say, you came all this way with no money?"

"I sort of figured to make a killing here," Sam told him.

Quirt studied Sam arrogantly, one foot balanced on the edge of the homemade table. He spoke with his flat, midwestern drawl. "How'd you come by that scar, Simmons?"

"I cut myself shaving," Sam told him.

Quirt found no humor in the remark. "You must have a shaky hand."

"Maybe I got a sharp blade," Sam replied. "How'd you lose that finger—picking your nose?"

Quirt flared with anger. He pushed away from the table and rose, drawing back his quirt.

Sam grabbed Quirt's wrist. He twisted Quirt around, put a foot in the small of his back, and kicked him, sprawling, into the wall, knocking over a table and some chairs in the process.

On the floor, Quirt shook his head. He went for his pistol. Then he stopped.

Sam had drawn first. His .45 was pointed and cocked.

Quirt relaxed his gun hand. He stood. "We ain't finished," he warned Sam, rapping his quirt against his thigh. "Not by a long shot."

"I'll be here," Sam told him.

Quirt pushed past Sam and left the cantina.

CHAPTER 7

SAM DIDN'T STAY LONG AT THE CANTINA. HE came back to the old church sacristy. Outside, the music and dancing continued, punctuated by laughter and the occasional firing of revolvers into the air.

Sam decided to go after Crawford tonight. He probably wouldn't get a better chance. Most of the scalp hunters would be dead drunk, sleeping it off. He would wait until the fandango ended and the promontory was quiet. That would be toward dawn. Then he would sneak into the hut used by Crawford and Teresa.

Teresa—what was he going to do about her? He didn't know. He'd kill her if he had to, but he hoped it didn't come to that. He'd have to play it by ear.

He sighed. Sometimes he wondered what he might have become if his parents hadn't been killed by Indians. He wondered what he might have been if the uncle who had taken him in had been a normal person, instead of an alcoholic who tried to rape his own sixteen-year-old daughter.

Would he be a cattleman, perhaps? A devoted husband and father? A respected member of the community?

Instead, he was a hunter of men, a killer, disliked on both sides of the law.

He had to admit, he had a talent for the job.

He lit the stub of a candle and started to unbuckle the straps of his bedroll. Then he stopped.

Someone had been through his things. They'd done a good job, but he could tell. The bedroll straps weren't quite the way he had left them. He opened his saddlebags. They had been gone through, as well.

He looked around. He was alone, or seemed to be. There was nothing in his saddlebags that would say he wasn't who he claimed to be. He kept the warrant on Crawford—it was a federal warrant, and he'd need it when he brought in the body—in his shirt. Still, this meant that somebody was watching him. They probably had an eye on him right now. Quirt Evans was the obvious choice, but it could be any of them.

Sam swore to himself. He would not be able to move against Crawford tonight. It was too dangerous. He would have to win the scalp hunters' trust. He would have to bide his time and prove himself to them. Sam had learned patience from the Apaches, but it was still not a virtue that came easily to him.

Sam took off his Apache moccasins and shell belt. Placing his pistol by his side, in case he should need it during the night, he wrapped himself in his blankets and went to sleep.

The next few days on the promontory were quiet, even dull. The men were restless, waiting for Perico to get back. They lazed around, drinking and playing cards. Some practiced target shooting or raced horses in the valley. There were occasional fights. The women, when they weren't drinking with the men, tended the crops and cattle. Sam saw little of Crawford. The scalp hunters' leader spent most of his time with Teresa. Quirt Evans was around, though—too much. Sam kept to himself and tried to blend in.

On the second day, Sam took the sorrel gelding out for some exercise. Working the horse hard, he rode it miles down the valley, far from the promontory. He needed to get away from those people. When he was done, he walked the lathered animal to cool it down.

He stopped in the cool shade of some giant

old cottonwoods that grew along a bend in the stream. He watered the horse there.

Suddenly, the hair on the back of his neck rose. He felt a chill.

He drew his rifle from its saddle scabbard. He left the horse by the stream, and he stepped noiselessly backward into the trees.

A few minutes later, a rider emerged from around the bend. It was Teresa.

Sam stepped into her path, rifle leveled.

"Oh," Teresa said, startled. She reined in her horse.

"Morning, ma'am," said Sam.

"Good morning," she replied, recovering.

Sam lowered the rifle. "Sorry if I scared you."

"Are you always so . . . vigilant?"

"It pays to be vigilant, ma'am, if you want to stay alive." Sam looked behind her. "Where's the colonel?"

Teresa laughed. "Recovering. Too much of the drink."

"Seems like he does a lot of that. Drinking and recovering, that is."

Her laughter took on a sad tinge. "Yes. More than he should. And it grows worse, I fear."

A stray beam of sunlight peeked through the trees and glinted off the gold cross around Teresa's neck. Sam could see now that she had been crying. She was not like the rest of the women up here, who looked hard as nails. There was a softness, a gentleness about her.

She said, "You won't shoot me, if I dismount?"

"No, ma'am."

"You do not have to call me 'ma'am.' My name is Teresa."

"All right—Teresa."

Sam held her horse while she swung down, her tiered jewelry tinkling musically. He let go of the animal, which joined his own at the stream. "What brings you so far from the mission?" he asked.

"Actually, I was looking for you."

"For me? Why?"

"To talk." Her dark eyes looked into his, unsettling him. "You intrigue me, Mr. Simmons—if that is your real name."

Sam raised his eyebrows. "If I'm going to call you Teresa, you better call me Sam."

Teresa smiled and went on. "That scar on your face, it says you have led a life of danger, but you do not seem the type man to make a living by taking human scalps."

What I really do isn't a hell of a lot different, Sam thought. But he said, "I do what I have to, to get by."

Teresa wouldn't accept that. "These men here, they are evil. They are monsters, some of them, especially Quirt Evans. They kill without remorse. But you have goodness in you. I can see that. I can feel it."

Sam scratched the back of his head. "You're one of the few people who's ever said *that,*" he admitted.

"What *do* they say about you?"

"Things it ain't polite to repeat around a lady."

She brightened. "And you think I am a lady?"

"Yes, ma'am. I do."

She smiled at him. Their eyes met again, and there was a tingling along the backs of his hands.

"No one has ever said that about me," she told him. She sounded like it was the nicest thing that had ever happened to her, and maybe it was.

Sam said, "Colonel Crawford, he doesn't feel that way?"

She lowered her eyes. "Sadly, no."

"I'm sorry." He didn't know what else to say.

Teresa shrugged, the shrug of a person who is resigned to disappointment.

Sam said, "How'd you and the colonel get hooked up, anyway?"

"The Apaches were responsible. They raided my village, in Mexico. It was a vengeance raid, for something my people had done to them. They killed everyone they could catch. I was the only one who got away. Thomas and his men, they found me. Some of the men, like Quirt and Slocum, they wanted to have their way with me, but Thomas would not let them. He could not leave me alone in that country. So he brought me back here with him."

"And you became attracted to him?"

"I had no choice. Thomas is educated and clever. He is kind, too, when he is not . . . not drinking."

"And when he is drinking?"

She didn't answer.

Sam said, "Does he leave you often? I mean, the way he had when I met him?"

"Often enough. I know he has his fancy women in Santa Fe. I know I don't measure up to them. I know that one day he will leave me and not come back. And yet . . ."

"And yet you wait for him."

She lowered her eyes. "Like I said, I have no choice. I have nowhere else to go."

"Do you love him?"

She looked up, and her eyes met his again, as if searching for something in his gaze. "No," she said at last. "I feel badly. Thomas and I are living in sin, not married. It is against all I was ever taught. Perhaps someday Thomas will take me away from this. Perhaps . . . perhaps someone else will."

Her voice had fallen low. She was very close to him. The smell of her perfume was like an intoxicant. They were far from the promontory, far from any prying eyes. It would be easy to take her into his arms. Sam had been a long time without a woman, and this one was damned attractive. But alarm bells were going off inside his head. He wondered if this was some kind of trap, if she was setting him up. Was she the one who'd gone through his things? If he wanted to make himself trusted by the scalp hunters, going after the leader's girlfriend was a hell of a stupid way to start.

Teresa solved his dilemma. She put a soft hand alongside his head. "Sam," she murmured. "I like that name." Then she raised up on tiptoe and kissed him.

Sam couldn't help himself. He was borne away on a sudden wave of passion. He returned her kiss, tenderly at first, then fierce and hard. She matched him. The patch of woods seemed to be spinning about them, as he bore her to the ground . . .

Afterward, he held her and stroked her glossy hair. He felt guilty about what he had done. She was like a scared, trapped animal, desperate for love and going after it the only way she knew how. She deserved a better man than Sam.

Two days ago, he had been ready to kill her if she got in his way. And now?

And now, he had compromised himself more than a man in his position ever should have.

His musings were interrupted by shots from the distant promontory. Teresa sat up in his arms. They both looked down the valley, though they were too far away to see anything.

"What is it?" Sam said.

"There is only one thing it can be," Teresa replied, and she looked at him sadly, because she knew he would soon be leaving. "It is Perico. He has found Nanay's camp."

CHAPTER 8

THE COLUMN OF MEN WOUND THROUGH THE rugged fastness of the Sierra Negros. The narrow trail was surrounded by steep, pine-clad ridges and jutting boulders. The crisp coolness of the mountains was a welcome relief from the torrid heat of the desert.

It was late afternoon. The men had been riding since dawn. There were twenty-two of them. They were armed with rifles and sawed-off shotguns. Almost all carried two pistols. If they had been drunk and lazy in camp, they were sober and alert now. Their lives depended on it.

They rode in single file, with their equipment tied down. There was no talking. Thomas

Crawford was in the lead. Somewhere ahead of him was Perico, riding point. Two more men rode rear guard. They were in Mexico, now. They had to be on the lookout for *rurales* as well as Apaches, though the likelihood of running into Mexican forces in this wild country was unlikely.

Quirt Evans was behind Crawford. Sam Slater followed behind Quirt. Sam's every nerve was alive. This was Apache country. He had ridden these mountain trails before, but in far different circumstances. He had been an Apache then, a *yodascin*, an adopted captive of the tribe. These jutting, pine-clad mountains brought back memories of happier days.

Sam didn't want to be here with these men. He'd had no choice but to come with them, though. He was supposed to be a member of the band. Maybe he should pull out, he thought. Maybe he should give up his plan to kill Crawford. But Sam was not the type to give up on anything. Anyway, it was too late now.

If nothing else, he was glad to get away from the abandoned mission, and from Teresa. The girl troubled him, as did his relationship with her. She had cried when they'd parted, before riding back to the promontory. Sam wasn't a man for romantic entanglements, and he was afraid that she had the wrong idea about him. He wished like hell that he had kept his hands off her.

At the head of the column, Crawford raised a hand. The men halted. Weapons ready, their eyes searched both sides of the trail. An ambush in this country could be fatal.

Like a wraith, Perico appeared. He wore the same purple shirt, breechclout, and red headband. A Winchester repeating rifle was cradled in his left arm. He spoke in whispers with Crawford, then the two of them rode ahead.

The column emerged in silence. Horses' hoofs stamped the ground. Low whinnies were choked off by the riders. Then Crawford returned. He motioned the men forward. Ahead, Sam heard the tinkling of a bell. He heard a dog barking.

The column emerged into a mountain glade. The bright green of the grass was all the more startling because they had not seen it in so long. Wildflowers dotted the glade in splashes of red and yellow.

Farther up the glade was a flock of white sheep, guarded by a mongrel dog that barked at the newcomers. On one side of the meadow was a wooden hut. In front of it, three children—two girls and a boy—were kicking an old tin can. A heavy-set woman rolled tortillas on a flat stone. The children stopped playing and looked at the strangers with curiosity. The woman stood, worried by the sight of so many heavily armed men.

Down the hill came the shepherd. He wore ragged pants and *guaraches*—Mexican sandals. A straw hat hung behind his head by a cord. The mongrel dog came with him, growling at

Crawford and his men. The hair on the dog's back stood up in warning.

The shepherd saw the column's Indian scout. He thought these must be gringo soldiers in civilian clothes, crossing the border after Apaches, as had happened several times before.

"*Buenos dias, señores,*" he said, smiling and revealing a mouth missing half its teeth.

Crawford nodded politely. "*Buenos dias.*" He motioned to Perico, who rode ahead. Quirt eased his horse alongside Crawford's. A sawed-off shotgun lay across Quirt's lap.

Crawford spoke to the shepherd in passable Spanish. "We're looking for Apaches. Are there any around?"

The shepherd waved his arm. "*Mas alla,*" he said, meaning, "farther on." "*Mas alla.*"

Crawford nodded and looked around. The dog watched the unfamiliar men from a crouch, still growling. Crawford said, "Are you all alone up here, *amigo?*"

The shepherd shrugged. "*Sí.* We travel with the seasons. We come here for the hot months. In the cold times, we go down below."

"You don't worry about the Apaches?"

"No, *señor.* We know them. They visit us from time to time. We give them a sheep—or they steal it. But they do not bother us."

"You're lucky."

"I don't know about that, *señor.* We put our trust in the Lord. It is all that a man can do."

Crawford said, "There is no one else with you?"

"No, *señor*. My brother, he used to travel with us, but he married a girl from Oputo. She did not like our life, I think, and now he owns a cantina there."

Crawford laughed. "Then he's even luckier than you are." He turned. "All right, boys."

As he spoke, Quirt lifted the shotgun and fired both barrels into the shepherd's chest. There was an instant of startled surprise in the shepherd's eyes, then he was blown across the clearing, with the upper half of his body torn apart.

At that moment, the dog snarled. It launched itself into the air, sinking its teeth into Quirt's left arm, knocking him from the saddle onto the ground.

The shepherd's wife dropped her tortillas in the dirt. She started instinctively for her children. "Run, *niños*!" She was ridden down from behind by a laughing scalp hunter. He fired a pistol into her back, and she sprawled forward, flopping in the long grass.

Quirt and the dog rolled on the ground. The dog tore at Quirt's arm. Yelling obscenities, Quirt managed to draw his knife from his belt. He plunged it into the dog's side. Again and again he struck, until the beast let go and dropped to its side on the ground, panting in its death throes.

The shepherd's three children ran for the safety of the pine forest. Yelling scalp hunters pursued them.

The boy stopped to cover his sisters. He had a sling. He put in a rock, swung it, and let go. The rock hit the first rider squarely between the eyes.

"Ow!" yelled the scalp hunter. He brought his horse to a halt and slumped forward in the saddle, holding his head. Blood trickled between his fingers. "Shit!" he said.

As the boy fitted another rock to his sling, the next scalp hunter rode by, shooting him twice with a pistol. The boy spun and fell on his back.

The youngest girl was running through the long grass when she was shot in the back of the head. She went down without a cry.

The oldest girl was twelve. She was tall for her age, just developing breasts. She had almost made it to the trees when she stepped in a hole in the ground and fell, twisting her ankle. She hobbled back to her feet, but before she could go farther, a lariat snaked around her shoulders and pulled tight. Slocum, the greasy-faced scalp hunter who'd thrown it, reined in his horse and took a turn around his saddle horn with the rope. Helpless, the girl stumbled and fell to her knees.

As she got up, Slocum threw himself from his saddle. He was a burly fellow, with a tobacco-stained shirt. His thick lower lip trembled as he ran up to the girl and lifted the rope from around her shoulders. She struggled, but he held her tightly. He ripped open the front of her cotton dress, revealing her budding breasts. With a little cry of delight, he pulled her to him, feeling her breasts and trying to kiss her.

"No!" said a voice from behind. It was Crawford.

Slocum looked up. The girl was scared. She looked up at Crawford as if he were a savior.

Slocum said, "But, Colonel . . ."

"She's a child, you fool," said Crawford.

"She looks like a woman to me," said Slocum. He turned back to her.

"I said *no!*" Crawford slipped a foot from the stirrup and kicked Slocum away from the girl. As she looked up in gratitude, Crawford leveled his pistol and shot her in the head. Her arms windmilled, and she fell backward onto the grass.

Slocum advanced on Crawford angrily. "You hadn't ought to have done that."

Crawford pointed the pistol at him. "You want some, too?"

Slocum glowered.

"Do you?" Crawford demanded. He was in a mood to pull the trigger.

Slocum got control of himself. He looked away. "No, Colonel," he said.

Crawford holstered his pistol. "We're not animals," he told Slocum.

The glade was quiet with the silence of death. The only sounds were the distant bell and faint bleating of the sheep. Thin wreaths of powder smoke drifted by and broke up on the breeze.

"Now, let's do what we came here for," Crawford said. He turned to Sam, all smiles again. "You're the new man, Sam. You want the first cut?"

Sam had watched the proceedings, helpless to interfere. He was no bleeding heart, but it was hard for him to pretend that he was not sickened by what he had seen. It was hard to look disinterested. He leaned on the saddle horn. "No, thanks," he said.

Quirt came up beside him, holding his chewed-up arm. There was blood on his wrist and both of his hands. He was in obvious pain as he turned to Sam. "How come you didn't help?"

Sam looked at him without expression. "I signed on to kill Apaches, not Mexicans."

"A scalp's a scalp."

Sam shrugged. "Maybe."

"Sure you ain't yellow?" Quirt asked.

"If I was you, I'd be more worried about that dog having rabies."

Quirt paled. Then he turned away, drawing his knife. The knife was still red with the dog's blood. Quirt said, "Well, I ain't too proud to lift a greaser scalp. Come on, boys."

The five bodies were scalped quickly, expertly. The circular scalps were stretched on little hoops of green wood to dry, then hung from the men's saddles.

Crawford was in high spirits as the men went about their grisly task. "Looks to me like we took an Apache warrior, his woman and three little ones—at least, that's what we'll tell the authorities in Hermosilio. This is just something to whet your appetites, boys. This is pocket change. The real payoff comes when we get Nanay."

Some of the men cheered.

"What'll we do with the bodies?" asked one man.

"Leave 'em," Crawford said. "Nobody comes this way, except Apaches. By the time the buzzards and coyotes do their work, nothing will be left of this bunch but the bones."

Just then, a scalp hunter wearing a battered plug hat emerged from the shepherd's hut. "Lookee what I done found," he crowed. He held up an earthen jug. "I do believe it's mescal."

Some of the men raised a cry. They got off their horses and started shoving for a turn at the jug, arguing with each other about who would drink first.

Crawford rode over. He halted the men by the tone of his voice. "Give me that," he ordered.

The men stopped their argument. The plug-hatted scalp hunter handed Crawford the jug.

"Hold out that arm, Quirt," said Crawford.

Quirt held out the arm that had been chewed by the dog. Crawford tipped the heavy jug and poured mescal over Quirt's wounds, cleaning them out, washing the blood away. Quirt bit back a howl of pain.

To the rest of the scalp hunters, Crawford said, "Are you people as stupid as you look? Have you forgotten everything I've taught you? Believe me, nobody wants a drink as much as I do. But what good are you going to be against the Apaches if you're drunk? You'll find yourselves being skinned alive, inch by inch."

He hurled the jug onto a rock, smashing it. The men watched sadly as the pale liquid drained into the earth. In a hurt voice, the man in the plug hat said, "Well, damn."

Crawford looked around. "Let's get going." To Sam, "Some of these people are impossible, but in this business I guess you can't expect much better."

The men mounted their horses, formed up, and rode off.

Sam rode just behind Crawford and Quirt Evans, who had wrapped a dirty bandana around his savaged arm. Sam was a hard man. He had seen a lot in his time, but nothing that had shocked him like this. And there was nothing he could do about it.

Yet.

CHAPTER 9

THE SCALP HUNTERS CAMPED THAT NIGHT IN the mountains. It was cold, but they built no fires. Jerky, hard biscuit, and corn dodgers were their meal. There was little conversation. Every man's nerves were on edge. They were deep in Apache country, where the penalty for failure was death.

Only Crawford was in high spirits. He had told Sam that he was addicted to danger. It was as if he enjoyed being in this situation. He saw to the guards and the horses. No detail escaped his notice. He patted men on the shoulder, cheering their spirits.

"How are you bearing up, Sam?" he asked,

just before they turned in.

"Well enough," Sam replied.

"No second thoughts about coming with us?"

"None," Sam lied.

"I didn't think you would have," Crawford said, and he flashed that boyish grin. "I've seen you in action."

Sam noticed Quirt Evans, off to one side, watching them.

Truth was, Sam had a lot of second thoughts about what he was doing, but he was in too deep to get out now. He wrapped himself in his blankets and went to sleep.

The next day, the country grew even wilder. At one point, the trail wound along a narrow ledge of rock. Below the column was a sheer drop of hundreds of feet. To their rear, a waterfall plunged out of a narrow gorge, spewing into a greenish pool far below. The thunderous din of the water echoed and re-echoed off the rocks.

In the afternoon, Perico bid them halt. "Not far, now," he told Crawford.

Guards were put out and the horses were picketed. The men grew increasingly nervous. Evans paced back and forth, tapping his leg with his quirt. His left arm was bandaged from the wrist to the elbow, where the shepherd's dog had chewed it. One man started to light a pipe, but Crawford snatched it from him.

"No," Crawford said. "Apaches can smell tobacco miles away."

After about an hour's wait, Crawford said, "Get ready, boys. From here, we go on foot."

The men left the horses in the care of a guard. "Check your weapons now," Crawford told them. "Be sure they're loaded and in good working order."

Quietly, the men checked rifles, shotguns, and pistols. They stuffed spare ammunition in their pockets. They sharpened knives on whetstones carried in their saddlebags. They took last bites of jerky or biscuit. They drank from their canteens.

"All right," said Crawford. He motioned with his arm. "Move out."

Crawford and Perico went first, followed by the others. Quirt Evans brought up the rear. They walked maybe three-quarters of a mile, climbing through groves of white oak and across a rock-strewn hillside. The late afternoon sun cast long shadows. They were high up; the rarefied air was chilly. Then they emerged onto a mountaintop plateau.

The view was breathtaking. Sam guessed he could see for a hundred miles, as wave after wave of rugged mountains receded into the distance. The blue sky was a giant bowl around them. Clouds scudded through it like great ships of war.

The plateau was level, or as close to it as anything they had seen in the last day and a half. It was open, broken here and there by clumps of oak, pine, and cedar. At the edge of the plateau was a gorge. The sheer rock walls at the far side of the gorge were already in shadow.

The small band of men was dwarfed by the immensity of the landscape, as they moved across the plateau. At the edge, Crawford waved them into line. They crept forward, into the cover of trees and rocks.

The walls of the gorge were not as steep on this side. Below, the gorge dropped into a rugged valley, bisected by a stream. Sand flats showed that the stream was shallow. Across the stream were Apache wickiups.

The valley was darkening. Fires had already been lit down there. Sam counted twenty-six wickiups.

"Call it a hundred and thirty people, altogether," Crawford whispered. "Big camp, for Apaches."

A drum started beating in the Apache camp, or *rancheria*. Even at this distance, the Indians looked extremely animated. Crouched beside Crawford, Perico muttered, "*Tulapai*."

Crawford nodded and grinned. "They're celebrating their raid. They're doing our work for us."

Tulapai was a fermented drink made from corn, a kind of beer. The Apaches drank it at big parties, along with *tiswin*, their other intoxicating drink, which was made from mescal. Men and women alike drank until they passed out. Drunken mothers even fed the liquor to their babies. These parties were frequently marred by fights, by killings, by riotous sex among people who were otherwise abstemious. Besides the violence, the use of the beverages led to indolence, bad nutrition, and poor health as a result of lying out drunk in all weathers. When the white men herded the Apaches onto reservations, the first practice they tried to stop was the brewing of *tulapai* and *tiswin*, and that prohibition was what angered the Apaches most at them. Many Apaches—Sam's adoptive father, Loco, among them—thought that *tulapai* and *tiswin* were the downfall of the tribe.

Sam looked on, sadly. He had seen his share of *tulapai* parties. He had seen good men turned into raving animals. He had seen men maimed and killed, women shamed, feuds started that lasted until one or both parties were dead, and were then carried into the next generation.

Crawford made himself comfortable in the rocks. "We'll let them get a snootful, then we'll go down and give them their haircuts. Perico, while there's still light, find us a way into that valley."

Perico moved off, carrying his rifle. More drums were beating below. Cries and songs filtered up to the men on the plateau. Sam could play this part only so far. The Apaches had been his brothers. He couldn't participate in their massacre. Neither could he stand by and watch, as he'd watched the killings of the shepherd and his family. He hadn't been prepared for those deaths; this time he knew what was coming. He had to warn the Indians. But how? He knew that some of the scalp hunters, especially Quirt, didn't trust him. He'd have to wait until dark and try to break away.

Dusk settled over the mountains. In the valley, the fires burned high. The drums beat loudly. Already men were dancing. It had been a successful raiding party. It was good to celebrate.

Sam was in a screen of pine trees. Slocum was beside him. With bad teeth, Slocum bit on a blackened fingernail as he watched the proceedings below.

"Big killing tonight, eh?" he said to Sam.

Sam grunted noncommittally.

Slocum pulled his knife from its sheath and ran a thumb along the edge. "A lot of work for this. You got you a good knife, Simmons?"

"Yeah," said Sam. He wished Slocum would shut up.

"You took scalps afore?"

"I've seen it done."

"Well, don't worry none. It ain't hard. It's fun, really, once you get the hang of it."

"I'm sure," said Sam.

"Your knife's gotta be sharp, that's the secret. Razor sharp. Takin' scalps with a dull knife is a pure pain in the ass. The other secret is, you don't want to cut too deep—remember that. But you also don't want to go too shallow. You got to get right under that hairline. You cut you a circle, or as good a circle as you can, and when you're done, you just take a hold and pull. You gotta pull hard, though. She won't come off, elseways. I like to brace my knees on the fella's shoulders, myself. 'Course, different folks got different ways."

Sam said nothing.

"You got any problems," Slocum said, "you just come to me."

"I intend to," Sam told him.

Sam looked away. He wondered who the real savages were.

As darkness fell over the mountains, Perico came back. He'd found a way down the gorge. Below, the drums thundered. The singing and dancing grew more frenzied. Shadowy figures could be seen staggering in front of the fires. There were wild cries. At the lip of the gorge, the scalp hunters waited. Some dozed off. By the time the dance was over, most of the Apaches would be passed out or too drunk to walk. They'd never stand a chance.

Sam wanted to sneak away, to get down the mountainside and warn the Apaches. But he couldn't leave before the others. He'd be missed. Crawford and his men would know who warned the Indians. Sam could escape their wrath, but it would mean leaving them free to commit more outrages, and that was something Sam did not want to do. It would also mean giving up his chance at the bounty on Crawford, and Sam didn't want to do that, either.

The hours dragged on. It grew cold atop the gorge. The trees and rocks offered little protection from the frigid wind. Around Sam, men shivered, complaining under their breaths. Sam waited quietly, motionless, like an Apache. It wasn't that Apaches didn't suffer from the elements like other men, it was that they were trained from childhood to endure hardship without complaint.

Finally, the word came. "Get ready to move."

The half-frozen men rose from their places. They stretched cramped muscles. They flapped their arms to warm up. Crawford passed down the line. "We're going down in single file. Don't lose touch with the man in front of you, or you might get lost. Worse yet, you might fall off this damn mountain. Keep your fingers off the triggers of those weapons. I don't want you accidentally firing and letting them know we're here."

They started off, with Perico leading the way. Sam was behind Slocum. A pimply criminal from New York, named Ripley, was behind Sam. In the darkness, the men moved downward, through the trees. They hadn't gone far when Sam silently slipped off to one side.

Sam heard Ripley mutter in surprise, then there was the sound of hurrying feet as the men behind Sam closed his break in the line.

Even before the last of the scalp hunters had gone past, Sam padded off to the right, circling around and ahead of them. There was a sling on his rifle, and he placed the weapon over his shoulders, giving him more freedom to use his hands.

He half threw himself down the steep hillside. He could climb or go down a mountain as well as any Apache, and he needed all of those skills now. He had to get to the bottom before the scalp hunters. The fires below provided vague illumination, outlining rock outcroppings and trees. He moved along the rock from ledge to ledge, praying that his next step did not launch him into space. He slid on the seat of his pants. He stubbed his toes on unseen rocks. He twisted an ankle. He tore the knee of his trousers and felt blood trickle down the inside of his leg. At one point, he lowered himself by the limb of a gnarled cedar. He took a step and suddenly found himself dangling, with nothing but air between him and the bottom of the gorge. Carefully, palms sweating, he worked himself back along the cedar limb until he found footing again. He rested there for a moment.

Then he turned his head. Had he heard noises behind him? Was he being followed? He listened but heard nothing more. It could have been a rabbit, or a mountain fox.

He kept going, moving left, sliding down the hill on his backside, feeling his way, working toward the fire-lit Apache camp. The throbbing of the drums and the wild keening of the singers provided accompaniment to his descent.

At last, he reached the bottom. His heart was pumping, but there was no time to rest. Before him, in the reflected light of the fires, he saw the stream and the mud flats. It would be safe to cross the stream there. Instead of firing shots, he would get close to the camp and shout a warning in Apache. Afterward, the scalp hunters would think that the Indians had discovered the white men's presence on their own. Or so Sam hoped.

He unslung his rifle and moved forward.

Suddenly, a shadowy form stepped into his path. "Going somewhere?" asked a voice.

It was Quirt Evans.

CHAPTER 10

QUIRT COVERED SAM WITH HIS RIFLE. Behind the two men, frenzied drumming mingled with dancing, singing, and drunken cries in the Apache village.

Sam caught his breath. "You'd have to be a good man to follow me down that hill."

"I am a good man," said Quirt in his flat, deadly voice. "I never trusted you, Simmons—or whatever your name is. I was watching you. I saw you drop out of line. I followed you, even though it damn near got me killed. Now, what's your game?"

Sam knew that as long as he could keep Evans talking, he had a chance to live. He said,

"I wanted to get down here early. Make sure I got my share. I wanted to be the one that got Nanay."

"Bullshit," Quirt said. "I can't figure you out, Simmons. You some kind of government agent or something? It's almost like you were trying to warn them Apaches."

"I'm a scalp hunter, same as you," Sam said.

"If you're a scalp hunter, I'm Buffalo Bill. I'd shoot you right now, but the noise would alert the Apaches and spoil the colonel's plan. Don't you worry, though. Soon as the colonel and the boys start their attack, you're going straight to hell."

Sam nodded over Quirt's shoulder. "Tell it to that Apache, right behind you."

Quirt laughed. "That's the oldest trick in the book. If you think I'd fall for that, you're even stupider than you look."

"Suit yourself," Sam said, still looking over Quirt's shoulder. "But in about two seconds, he's going to put an arrow in your back."

By the reflected light of the fires, Sam saw the slightest bit of hesitation on Quirt's face. Quirt sneaked a look over his shoulder. That was when Sam launched himself at the scalp hunter.

Quirt didn't shoot. He swung the stock of the rifle. Sam dodged reflexively. The blow glanced off the side of his head. It hurt like hell. Sam caught Quirt by the waist. Quirt kept smashing down at him with the rifle. Sam twisted Quirt around, grabbing a leg, dragging him to the ground. Quirt lost his rifle in the fall. He jumped on Sam, clawing at Sam's ear, trying to rip it off. Sam twisted Quirt's bandaged arm, the one mangled by the dog. Quirt groaned with pain, and his grip on Sam relaxed.

Sam shook Quirt off. He rolled away, stars still exploding in his eyes from the rifle blow on the side of his head. He tried to get up. Before he could, something was wrapped around his neck. It was Evans' quirt.

Evans twisted the braided leather around Sam's neck. Sam was on his knees. He tried to get his fingers between his neck and the quirt, but he couldn't. He pushed and pulled, trying to throw Evans off. He couldn't do that, either. He tried to hurt Evans' bad arm again, but this time Quirt fought through the pain.

The quirt dug deep into Sam's neck, strangling him. Sam lurched forward on his knees. He was in the muddy shallows of the river. He tried to stand, but Quirt held him down. The two men staggered around in an embrace of death.

Sam fought for air, trying not to black out. It was hard to keep his balance. His eyes clouded. There was one last move he could make. He went limp. The move threw Quirt momentarily off balance. That was enough for Sam to roll forward, ducking one shoulder and throwing Quirt over it.

Quirt hit the shallow water with a splash. He partially lost his grip on the quirt. Sam broke free. Gasping for air, he leaped on Quirt's back.

He pushed the scalp hunter's head beneath the shallow water, holding it down.

Quirt struggled. His feet scrabbled in the mud. His arms and hands flailed the water. Sam leaned on him with all his strength, for Quirt was a powerful man. Quirt tried desperately to raise his head, but he couldn't get it out of the mud.

Suddenly, Quirt's struggles ceased. A mass of bubbles rose to the surface of the water. Sam held Quirt there another minute, until he was convinced that the j30 was dead. He gave the head one last push, then he stood.

He was wet, muddy, exhausted. His neck was scraped raw; his head throbbed. His voice box felt like it was broken from the pressure of Evans' quirt. He fell back to his hands and knees in the water. He wanted to roll over and lay down, but he couldn't. He had to warn the village. He got back up. Then he stopped.

Across the stream, two people stood at the edge of the trees, watching him. They were Apaches.

It was a man and a woman. They must have come down here to be alone and heard the fight. They'd probably thought it was two drunken members of their tribe. Now they realized who it was they'd been watching.

Stumbling from the *tulapai* they had imbibed, the Apache couple turned and ran for the village.

"*Indah!*" the woman yelled. "*Indah!*"—"White man!"

Sam stood ankle deep in the stream. This was the best thing that could have happened.

"Indah!"

In the village, the drumming and singing came to a confused halt. The dancers stopped. *"Indah! Indah!"*

People began yelling, running in all directions.

From downstream came a volley of oaths, followed by Crawford's voice. "Come on, boys!"

Out of the shadows came the scalp hunters, in a ragged line. They pounded across the stream, yelling. They scrambled up the rocky slope on the other side. Somebody tripped, and his rifle went off.

"There's no time to surround the village," Crawford yelled. "We'll have to charge through!"

Then they were into the flat, open area used by the dancers. Rifles, shotguns, and pistols began to fire. There were yells and screams.

Many of the Apaches had continued to mill around the dance area in drunken confusion. These died quickly. Others ran—or stumbled—for the horses. Others sought refuge among the rocks and brush. Still others climbed the far side of the gorge. Some of the men stopped to fight, covering the retreat of their tribesmen with rifles and pistols, with bows and arrows.

Sam followed the scalp hunters into the *rancheria*, powerless to stop the slaughter. He heard women and children screaming, babies crying amidst the gunfire. The scalp hunters ran through the camp, shooting everyone they came to. Men and women were killed without mercy. They were shotgunned at close range. They were shot with rifles and pistols. Sam saw a small child, a toddler, trying to get away. She was shotgunned in the back by a man named Kingsley.

Everything was noise and confusion. Some of the brush wickiups had caught fire. Sam saw one of the scalp hunters spin and fall, clutching his throat.

"Find Nanay!" It was Crawford's voice. "Find Nanay, damn it! He's worth five thousand pesos!"

Sam looked around. It was like watching his own family being massacred. For a moment, he was ready to kill Crawford now, and take his chances. The hell with the reward. He heard Crawford's voice, but he couldn't find him in the confusion.

The Apaches who had stayed to fight were by the wickiups. They fought well, but they were overwhelmed by Crawford's men. In the heat of battle, men shot at each other point-blank. The wounded lay on the ground, firing pistols, all this in the hellish, blood-red light of the fires.

Then the last of the Apaches went down.

"Don't let any of them get away, men! They're money in your pockets!"

The scalp hunters charged past the wickiups into the brush, rooting out survivors. One of the gang ran by Sam with a dripping scalp in his hand. There was no one looking, so Sam shot him down. Grim satisfaction showed on Sam's face.

Apache women, children, and a few men were dragged out of the brush. Some were wounded. All were executed, and their bodies brought back to the *rancheria.* They were laid in the open area where, a short while before, they had been dancing. The rest of the Indian bodies were collected. From the close-in fighting, many of the scalp hunters were splashed with blood, brains, and bits of bone and hair.

When the last of the bodies had been brought in, it was nearly dawn. Crawford examined the haul by the fading light of the fires. Sam stood near him. The other scalp hunters were all around. Now that Sam had found Crawford, there was no way to get at him without committing suicide.

"Is that all of them?" Crawford asked.

"All we could find, Colonel," answered the greasy fellow called Slocum.

"There must be about eighty here. That means upwards of fifty got away. Looks like we lost most of the warriors, too. Damn, how did they know we were here? A few minutes more, and we'd have bagged them all. Damned bad luck. What were our casualties?"

"Two dead, five wounded, Colonel. Two of the wounded are hurt pretty bad," Slocum reported.

Crawford looked around. "Where's Quirt?"

"Dunno," said one of the scalp hunters. "Ain't seen him since we left the bluff."

"Quirt!" Crawford cried. "Quirt!"

There was no answer. Only the silence of death.

"Oh, well. He'll turn up," Crawford said. "He's probably got one of their women out there in the brush." He turned to Perico. "Did you find Nanay?"

"No," said the Chihenne Apache.

"What about you, Sam?" said Crawford.

Sam shook his head.

Crawford swore under his breath.

"Maybe he's in this bunch here," said Slocum. Many of the bodies were unrecognizable, because of their wounds. Others were piled one atop the other, like cordwood.

"He'd better be," Crawford replied. He looked at the sky. "It'll be getting light soon. All right, boys, get to work."

CHAPTER 11

AS GRAY DAWN FILTERED TO THE BOTTOM of the gorge, Crawford's men began scalping the dead Apaches.

Only about ten men got to do the actual scalping. The rest were needed for other duties. The scalpers pulled up the bodies one by one, like so many slaughtered cattle. With well-sharpened knives, they sliced under each dead Indian's hair and cut a circle around the crown of the head. Man, woman, or child, it made no difference—all were treated alike. When the circle was complete, the scalp hunter put down his knife, braced himself, and pulled. Usually, the scalp came away with a ripping or popping sound. The undersides were covered with blood and gobbets of flesh.

"Put the scalps in this sack," Crawford told the men, and he tossed them a leather bag. "There's no time to scrape and dry them. We'll do that later, after we get the horses and get out of here."

"What about the bodies?" asked one of the men, a lean Texan named Werdann. Like many of the scalp hunters, he was splashed with dried blood and gore from last night's massacre.

"Leave them for the buzzards," Crawford told him. "They're only Indians."

Crawford put out guards to watch for the return of the surviving Apaches, then he turned to Sam. In the darkness, he had not noticed the livid bruises that Quirt's rifle butt had left on Sam's face and the side of his head. Now he saw them, and he winced. "What happened to you?"

"What didn't?" Sam said.

"You look like you're lucky to still be with us."

If you only knew, Sam thought. He said, "I am. Real lucky."

Crawford flashed his boyish grin. "Well, outside of that, what did you think of your first action with us?"

Sam wished that he could tell Crawford what he really thought about his "action." He wished that he could put a bullet between the scalp hunter's eyes. But he had a role to play—for now. So he said, "A very professional job, Colonel."

"Too bad the savages were alerted, or our

haul would have been even greater." Crawford indicated the bodies stacked on what had once been the dance ground. "There's a lot of old men among them, aren't there? Indians all look alike to me, especially when they've had their heads blown open. Why don't you check through them, Sam. See if your friend Nanay is there. If he is, cut off his head and bring it to me."

"All right," Sam said. It gave him a way to avoid having to take scalps. He knew Nanay wouldn't be among the dead. Nanay wouldn't be caught that easily. He was too wily. If anyone got out of this slaughter, it would have been Nanay.

While Sam checked the bodies, Crawford ordered two more men to dig a grave for the pair of dead scalp hunters. One of the scalp hunters had been killed by Sam, but Crawford did not know that.

Then Crawford visited his wounded. Three of them had received minor injuries. A fourth had the lower part of his jaw shot away. Someone had bound the man's face with an old shirt, which was already soaked with blood.

Crawford knelt and patted the man's shoulder. "Take it easy, Paulsen. We'll get you out of here." There was no doctor at the mission; there was no doctor within two hundred miles. The odds on Paulsen surviving were a thousand to one, but Crawford did not tell that to the wounded scalp hunter.

The fifth man, a youngster named Childress, had been shot through the spine. He was paralyzed from the neck down. Crawford looked at him squarely. "There's no hope for you, Childress. You know that."

Childress blinked his eyes in scared recognition.

Crawford went on. "We can't take you with us. You'd never make it out of this gorge. And I won't leave you to be tortured by the Apaches."

Childress blinked again. There was resignation on his face, now.

Crawford pursed his lips. In a low voice, he said, "I'm sorry, son. I've got no choice." He stood and drew his pistol. He aimed it and shot the young scalp hunter in the head. The pistol's flat report echoed through the gorge, breaking the dawn stillness.

"Bury him with the rest," Crawford told the men working on the grave. He raised his voice to those who were taking scalps. "Hurry, you men. We can't stay here long. There's too many Apaches that aren't dead. They could come back at any time, and if they do, they won't be in a good mood."

"Colonel!" It was one of the guards, down by the stream. "Colonel, I found Quirt!"

Crawford walked over, making a point of not hurrying. Some of the other scalp hunters followed. Sam watched from where he had been looking for Nanay among the bodies. The guard stood next to Quirt, who lay facedown in the shallow water at the edge of the stream.

Crawford turned to those who had followed

him. "Get back to work. You've all seen dead men before."

Reluctantly, the scalp hunters trickled away. Crawford knelt and turned over Quirt's body. "He wasn't shot. There's bruises on his face, marks on the back of his neck. He was drowned. Drowned in one foot of water."

Crawford stood. "How did this happen? *When* did it happen? And why here? Was he killed before we even got to the village? But that doesn't make sense."

The guard said, "Maybe he chased one of them Apaches from the village this way during the fight, and got hisself drownded."

"Maybe," Crawford said, but his tone indicated that the explanation did not sit right with him. "It's strange that nobody saw him from the time we left the ridge." He sighed. "I guess we'll never know. Quirt won't tell us, that's for sure. Too bad. He was a good man."

At that moment, Sam came up. Crawford looked at him. "Well, Sam—did we get Nanay?"

Sam shook his head. "No. He must have gotten away."

"Son-of-a—" Crawford caught himself. He rubbed his unshaven cheek. "All right. There's nothing we can do about it. We've got a damned good haul even without Nanay. Get somebody to help you carry Quirt over to where they're digging that grave."

Sam nodded, and Crawford walked away.

Sam went back to the *rancheria,* where the

squad of men was still taking scalps. The scalpers' hands and sleeves were splashed with blood. The scout Perico, who as an Apache did not take scalps, stood off to one side, watching dispassionately.

Sam saw Ripley, the New Yorker who'd been beside him on the bluff. Ripley looked a bit ill. "Take a break," Sam told him. "The colonel wants somebody to help me carry Quirt to the gravediggers."

Ripley stood gratefully. He was a short, pinch-faced fellow. He wiped his bloody hands on his wool trousers. The two men went to the stream and lifted Quirt's body from the water.

"What do you think happened to him?" Ripley asked Sam.

Sam shrugged. "Maybe he couldn't swim."

They carried the body into the village. Ripley grimaced under his heavy load. "Could be, somebody had a score to settle with Quirt, and they thought this was a good time to do it."

"Could be," Sam said.

"Where did you go last night, Simmons? I lost you right after we started off. You look like you fell off the damn cliff."

Sam laughed, as if at himself. "I went the wrong way in the dark. I missed Slocum. Don't know how. I recovered, though, and caught up to the end of the line. I was right behind you when we went into the village."

"Man, we were lucky just to get to the village. You nearly got half the company lost."

"I know. Listen, do me a favor, will you, and don't tell the colonel. He'd skin me alive."

Ripley laughed. "Don't worry, I won't. Anyway, it worked out all right."

Sam wondered if anyone would associate his bruises with Quirt Evans' violent end. There was no reason for them to do so, and even if they did, they would assume it was the settling of a personal grievance—Quirt and Sam were known to dislike each other—and they would leave it at that.

Sam and Ripley left Quirt's body with the gravediggers. Then they went back to where the scalpers were performing their grisly task. Sam swore to himself that, no matter what, he would not cut hair from one of the dead Indians.

"How many did you kill?" Ripley asked.

Sam grunted. "I don't know. My share, I guess."

"Man, that was some turkey shoot. You took any scalps yet?"

"No. The colonel's kept me busy."

"I noticed that. The colonel's took a real shine to you. Wouldn't surprise me, you ended up with Quirt's job."

"Whatever the colonel wants," Sam said. "He's the boss."

As they returned to what had been the dance area, Ripley pulled his knife. "Want to trim some hair with us?"

"No. The colonel told me to report back to him."

He left the New Yorker. He needed a way to avoid helping with the scalps, so he went back to the gravediggers. They had laid Quirt in the common grave, atop their other three dead companions. Sam said, "I'll finish up here. Colonel said for you boys to get some scalps."

"Thanks, Simmons," the gravediggers said, and they left.

Sam filled in the grave. He was no nearer a solution on how to dispose of Crawford then he had been when he'd met him on the edge of the *Jornada*, and that rankled him. So far, all he'd done was waste time—and watch a lot of innocent people die.

Crawford came by. He'd been searching what remained of the wickiups for anything of value. He hadn't found much—a bit of Mexican and American money, women's jewelry, a watch. Some of the Apache horses remained, but they weren't worth taking. "How are we doing?" he said.

Slocum, who seemed to enjoy his work, held up a bloody treasure. "Here's the last of them, Colonel."

"Good," said Crawford. "What's the count?"

"Eighty-three," said the Texan, Werdann, hefting the leather sack. "You guessed it right close, Colonel."

Crawford nodded. "One of our best hauls yet. If only we'd gotten Nanay. All right, Mr. Slocum. Call in the guards. Get the wounded on their feet. Form up, and let's be on our way."

Slocum nodded. He moved around the perimeter of the village, cupping his hands and shouting, "Guards in! Guards in!" Meanwhile, the rest of the scalp hunters lined up. The three lightly wounded men were assisted to their feet. Paulsen, the man with the jaw shot off, was supported between two of his fellows. Crawford carried the sack of scalps.

As the men lined up, they shuffled across the grave of their dead fellows. By doing that, they hoped to obliterate the grave's traces, so that the Apaches would not discover it and dig up the four bodies that were buried there.

"Everyone here?" Crawford asked Slocum.

"All but Robertson, Colonel. He was posted out to the west, just beyond that brush there."

Slocum advanced in the direction of the guard post. "Robertson!" he called. "Robertson, what the hell are you doing out there?"

There was no answer. Crawford looked worried.

Slocum advanced a few steps more. "Robertson! That son-of-a-bitch better not be asleep."

"Here he comes," cried one of the scalp hunters near the end of the line.

Robertson walked into the village. There was a strange stiffness to his gait. His rifle was missing.

Slocum said, "Robertson, did you get into the *tulapai?* What the hell is . . ."

Then he stopped. Robertson half turned, revealing a two-foot arrow in his back. He pointed in the direction from which he'd come. He said, "The Apaches. They're . . ."

Then he collapsed in the dirt.

Crawford didn't need to see any more. "The Apaches are back," he cried. "Let's get moving."

CHAPTER 12

THE SCALP HUNTERS RETREATED ACROSS the river. Led by the renegade Perico, they reclimbed the gorge. Shots rang out behind them. Bullets smacked into the gorge's rock walls. The Apaches were considered the best shots of all the Indian tribes, and the gunfire made the fleeing scalp hunters move even faster.

"Don't panic, men," cried Crawford. "That's what they want. Keep together."

The men were tired and hungry, but they kept on, propelled by fear. A pair of them helped Paulsen, the man with the shattered jaw. They reached the top with no casualties. They began to run across the open plateau.

"Stay in line, damn you!" Crawford commanded. "You're not rabble."

Reluctantly, they obeyed him. Like the others, Sam's heart was in his mouth as they neared the dip where the horses had been left. He expected to find the guard dead and the horses gone.

But the horses were there, hobbled out to graze. The guard was relieved to see the returning men. "Thank God you're back, Colonel. Hot damn, but I was getting spooked. I heard all them shots and . . ."

"Have the horses been fed?" Crawford demanded.

"Yes, sir. First thing this morning, just like you said."

Crawford turned. "All right, boys. Get your gear and saddle up. Don't waste time doing it, either."

The men did not need to be told that last part. They threw saddles and bridles on their horses. Crawford hung the leather bag full of scalps from his saddle horn. Paulsen and the other wounded were helped to mount.

"Everybody ready?" Crawford cried. "Let's ride."

The scalp hunters started off. Perico led the way. The others followed at as quick a gait as they could maintain in this rough country. There was a sense of frightened haste, and only Crawford's presence kept the retreat from turning into a rout.

Around them, the mountains and forest grew

unnaturally quiet. The men were anxious. They looked around as they rode, fingers on the triggers of their weapons. There had been no more shots since they had reached the plateau at the head of the gorge. The Apaches seemed to have vanished.

"Where did they go?" whispered Ripley, in front of Sam.

"Don't worry," Sam told him. "They're out there."

The trail took them once more along the narrow ledge of rock by the waterfall. Paulsen, the man with the shattered jaw, had trouble staying conscious. He nodded off for a second, slumped in his saddle, and almost fell off. He recovered, grabbing his horse's reins in panic, causing the animal to lose its footing on the narrow ledge. Man and horse teetered for a second, as if in suspended animation, then they toppled over and fell. They arced outward into the air, curved back in and bounced off the rock walls, then continued their plunge to eternity. Their screams were drowned out by the thunder of the waterfall.

The scalp hunters watched, mesmerized.

"Hell of a way for a man to learn he can't fly," Sam remarked.

The column continued on.

Sam wondered what would happen if Nanay found him with the scalp hunters. Nanay would think that Scar, the *yodascin*, had turned against his adopted people. He would think that Scar had betrayed them for the white man's money, the same as Perico. Only in Sam's case it would be worse, because Sam's adoptive father had been a great chief and war leader of the Chiricahua. He wondered what they would do to him if they took him alive.

He bet it wouldn't be pretty.

Deep in the mountains, the column stopped. They were at the entrance to a narrow defile, one of many they must pass through on their way back to their base at the mission. The defile's steep sides were a mass of pine trees and jagged boulders. The quiet was almost deafening.

Up front, Perico looked from side to side, his handsome face searching the rugged slopes.

Ripley said, "I don't like this, Simmons. I don't like it at all."

"I ain't real thrilled with it, myself," Sam replied. The hair on the back of Sam's neck was standing straight up. There were chills up and down his spine.

Slocum was in front of Ripley. Sweat and dirt were beaded on Slocum's greasy face. He tried to wipe them off, but that gesture only spread the mess around worse than it had been.

Crawford rode forward and came alongside Perico. "See anything?" he asked the renegade Apache in a low voice.

Perico shook his head, once. "No."

Crawford looked behind him. He didn't like this, either. He knew that Apaches could travel faster on foot in these mountains than white men could on horseback. "We have no choice," he said at last. "We can't go back. We have to go on."

He waved the column forward.

The scalp hunters entered the defile. The only sound was the clopping of their horses' hoofs on the rocky ground.

At the top of the slope, an eagle suddenly took flight, its giant wings outstretched.

In front of the column, Perico turned in his saddle to shout a warning. There was a rifle shot, and Perico toppled from his horse.

Two more shots sounded at the rear of the column. The rear rider was down, as well, thrashing on the ground in pain, blocking the exit to the narrow pass.

Crawford turned. He yelled something, but his voice was drowned out, as giant boulders came crashing down both sides of the defile. Some of the huge rocks shattered. Others gathered headway, making a thunderous noise in the confined area. They bounced in the air and smashed into the column of scalp hunters. In front of Sam, one of the giant rocks hit Ripley and his horse, turning them into a gelatinous pulp. Rifle fire began pouring down on the white men. Horses reared. Men cried out and fell.

"Ride through!" Crawford yelled. "Don't stop!"

The scalp hunters tried to escape. Everything was confusion, with men being hit and riderless horses running loose. Smoke from rifles mixed with dust kicked up by the falling boulders.

Sam made for the far end of the defile. He had to go slowly. Men and horses were down everywhere, and the terrain was bad. He passed a scalp hunter whose leg had been caught beneath one of the boulders. The man lay screaming in agony, trying to extricate his crushed leg.

Sam snapped a couple of pistol shots up the hillside. There was no chance of hitting anyone—not one Apache had been seen since the fight had started—but it might make the Indians keep their heads down. Gunfire echoed off the sides of the pass, along with the screams of men and animals. Ignoring Crawford's orders, a group of terrified scalp hunters had dismounted and were trying to make a stand. Sam saw one go down, shot in the face. Ahead, he thought he glimpsed Crawford escaping from the constricted passage.

Sam came to the place where Perico had been shot. Another man and two horses had gone down here, as well, causing a panicked jam on the narrow trail. Sam kicked his horse up the steep side of the defile and went around them. Bullets hummed so close to his ears that he could almost feel them brush by. Other bullets whined off nearby rocks.

Then Sam was around the jam and through the defile, onto what passed for open ground in these mountains. Just then, his horse was hit by an Apache bullet. The animal reared and fell, throwing him.

Sam hit the ground heavily. Stunned, he lay there for a second, then he tried to get up. He staggered around, unsteady on his feet, his balance affected by the force of the fall. His horse was dead. He looked back at the defile. Most of the scalp hunters back there were dead. The Apaches were moving out of the rocks, now. They were running, coming for him.

Sam fumbled the rifle from his saddle scabbard. He couldn't outrun the Apaches. He'd have to sell his life as dearly as possible. He knew one thing—they weren't going to take him alive.

The Apaches yelled as they drew close. Then, behind Sam, there were hoofbeats. Sam turned and saw Crawford riding toward him, bent low over his horse's neck, firing his pistol at the oncoming Apaches.

The Indians slowed for a second, surprised by this new development. They began firing at Crawford. Crawford reined in his horse alongside Sam. He slipped a foot from the stirrup and offered Sam a hand.

"Get on!" he cried.

Sam put his foot in the stirrup and swung up behind the scalp hunter. Behind them, the Apaches came on again. Both Sam and Crawford fired at them. One of the Indians stumbled and sprawled on his face. Then Crawford kicked his horse and rode away. Behind them, they heard gunfire and the screams of the dying.

When they were out of the Apaches' range,

Crawford slowed his horse. Ahead, the few survivors of the scalphunting expedition waited for them.

"That's twice you've saved my life," Sam told Crawford.

The scalp hunter grinned over his shoulder. "What are friends for?"

CHAPTER 13

BESIDES SAM AND CRAWFORD, ONLY THREE scalp hunters had survived the Apache ambush—Slocum, the lean Texan Werdann, and a sullen-looking fellow called Kingsley. They were all shaken. Kingsley wrapped a strip of cloth around his forehead, where it had been creased by an Apache bullet. Blood had gotten all over his face, and he wiped it off with his shirttail. Slocum's greasy face was sweatier than ever. He was so scared, he could barely hold onto his horse's reins.

"There's no sense hanging around," Crawford told them. "It won't do those poor bastards back there any good. Let's go, before Nanay comes after us."

He turned. "Sam, you comfortable back there?"

"More comfortable than I would have been if the Apaches had gotten me," Sam said.

Crawford waved a hand, and the five men rode off. Crawford was a strange fellow, Sam thought. He didn't have to let Sam share his horse and put an extra strain on the animal. A lot of men would have dumped Sam, ridden off, and saved themselves. Sam might have done it himself.

The riders hurried, fearful of Apache pursuit. At each bend in the trail, at each mountain pass, the men went cold, thinking this was where they might be ambushed again. But nothing happened.

Night came, and the little group made camp. There was no fire. Supper was cold jerky and water from their canteens. Slocum was so hungry that he ate some of his horse's grain. The guard rotation was set. Sam and Crawford were nervous enough, but the other three men were terrified. Sam was afraid they would open up at some forest noise or shadow in the dark and alert the Apaches to their whereabouts.

At last, it was Sam's turn for guard.

It was the darkest hour of the night. Nothing moved, save those predators who inhabited the world of darkness. The exhausted scalp hunters slept.

Sam made the rounds of the camp. All was quiet. Sam drew his pistol and cocked it.

He would kill all of them before they knew what was happening. He would get their bodies back to civilization and collect sixty-five hundred dollars. Sam moved silently to where Crawford slept. He pointed the pistol at the sleeping man. His finger curled on the trigger.

Then he lowered the weapon.

His chest was heaving. Sweat beaded on his unshaven lip.

He couldn't do it.

Was it because Crawford had twice saved his life? He didn't know. Those acts didn't excuse the monstrous deeds the scalp hunter had performed. Was it because he couldn't kill a man—even a man like Crawford—in cold blood? He didn't know that, either. He just knew that he couldn't go through with it. He wished he had never come on this job. He wished he had never heard of Thomas Crawford and his scalp hunters.

He let down the pistol's hammer. He holstered the weapon and went back on guard. He didn't know whether he had done the right thing or not.

The night passed without attack, but Apaches did not usually attack at night. Just at dawn, that was their favorite time. Crawford had the surviving scalp hunters awake well before then. They formed a perimeter around their little camp, nervous, weapons loaded and ready.

The minutes crawled by. No shots were fired at the men. No Apaches appeared.

Crawford held them there until the sun peeped over the horizon. "Let's go," he said cautiously.

The men grained, watered, and saddled their horses, while Sam, who was without a horse, kept watch. When all were ready, they moved out.

They rode all day, passing the meadow where the shepherd and his family had been killed. Vultures and coyotes had already been at work on the bodies.

"Funny, isn't it?" Crawford said. "We went to all that trouble to kill those people, then we lost their scalps."

"We did?" said Slocum.

Crawford laughed. "Yes. Quirt and some of the other men were carrying them. Oh, well. Easy come, easy go." He tapped the leather sack that hung from his saddle horn. "We've more than enough here to make up for them—and a hell of a lot less people to split the money with." He laughed again, heartily.

In the afternoon, the little group of men descended into their home valley. The promontory with the abandoned mission was visible in the distance. The scalp hunters halted in relief, feeling safe at last.

Crawford said, "We'll stay here the night, long enough to get our women and refresh the horses. Then we're pulling out."

"Pulling out?" asked Slocum in disbelief.

"That's right. The scalp hunters are disbanded, gentlemen. We'll split our take, then it's every man for himself, and it's been nice working with you."

"But why?" said the sullen-faced Kingsley.

"Nanay lost most of the women and children in his band. That can't make him happy. He's going to come after us, and he isn't going to stop until he's killed us."

Werdann, the Texan, said, "But we've got the mission. We can hold it against the Indians, can't we?"

Crawford said, "With twenty-five men we could hold that promontory against an army. With five, we can't hold it against the Ladies' Aid Society. Even if we could, we don't have enough men for any more scalphunting raids. Nope, boys, it's all over. Time to find ourselves another line of work."

He turned to the man who shared his horse. "Sorry, Sam. I hope you got your revenge against the Apaches this time out, because it looks like there won't be any more."

Sam thought about Quirt, and about the other man he had killed at the Apache *rancheria*. He thought about all the scalp hunters whose deaths he was indirectly responsible for. "I did all right," he said.

"We going to Hermosilio to sell our scalps?" asked Slocum.

Crawford shook his head. "My first goal is to put daylight between us and Nanay. Hermosilio is back the way we just came. I plan to cross the

Jornada, then take the long way round, through Yuma, Puerto Penasco, and down the Gulf of California by boat. That agreeable to everybody?"

Slocum, Kingsley, and Werdann looked at each other and nodded. Crawford said, "Sam?"

Sam nodded assent. He was washing his hands of this business. Like Crawford, he had decided to move on to other things.

The men rode to the mission. It was a quiet group of women and hangers-on that turned out to greet them, as they crossed the causeway onto the promontory. Already, some of the women had started to sob. They knew what had happened without being told. Teresa walked beside Crawford's horse, but she had eyes only for Sam. Her face was filled with relief that he had come back alive.

They rode through the gate, into the mission yard. They halted in front of the old church. As they did, a man stepped out of the shadowed church doorway. The man was huge; he was built like a beer barrel with a head. He wore eyeglasses, and his hair was done in a long blond pigtail that reached nearly to his waist. He carried a Smith & Wesson hunting rifle, and the rifle was trained on Sam.

"Hello, Slater," he said.

CHAPTER 14

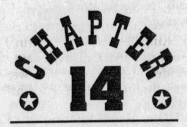

SAM RECOGNIZED THE HUGE MAN. HE WAS the one who had tracked Sam and Crawford across the *Jornada.* There was a faded bloodstain on his shirt. He must have gotten that in the encounter at Dead Man's Tanks.

"I thought you were dead," Sam said.

"Life's full of surprises, ain't it?" said the big man. "Get your hands up, Slater." He motioned with the rifle. "Get 'em up, I said."

Sam obeyed. What choice did he have?

Crawford recognized the big man, too. "Why do you keep calling him Slater?" he asked.

" 'Cause that's his name. Sam Slater."

A strange look came over Crawford. "The one they call The Regulator?"

"That's him."

Crawford turned to Sam. "Is that true?"

Sam tried to brazen it out. "No. My name's Sam Simmons. I don't know who this long-haired clown is, but he's got me mixed up with somebody else."

Behind the glasses, the big man's eyes gleamed. "The name's Honeycutt, Slater, and I ain't got you mixed up with nobody. I been trackin' you a long time. I been wantin' you."

Crawford said, "You mean it was Sam you were after in the *Jornada,* and not me?"

Honeycutt kept his eyes, and the rifle, on Sam. "That's right."

Crawford's voice was not as friendly as it had been. "Better get off your horse, Sam, till we get this cleared up. Keep the hands up, if you don't mind."

Sam swung one leg over his saddle horn. He took his other foot from the stirrup and dropped to the ground.

The rest of the scalp hunters dismounted. Crawford nodded to Slocum. "Search him."

Slocum said, "I thought you searched his stuff once before."

"Not his clothes, I didn't," Crawford told him. "Go ahead."

Methodically, Slocum went through Sam's clothing. At last, he found the warrant hidden inside Sam's shirt. He read the document—the few words that he could understand—then he handed it to Crawford.

Crawford read it. He looked at Sam. "You're carrying a federal warrant with my name on it. Why?"

"Something to read when I'm in the latrine?"

"Don't get smart," said Werdann. He rapped the side of Sam's head with his rifle butt. Sam saw stars. He fell to his hands and knees.

To Honeycutt, Crawford said, "You're sure this is Sam Slater?"

"Ain't no mistaking that scar," Honeycutt said. "Or that busted nose. It's Slater, all right."

Crawford looked at Sam. "To return to my question. Logic suggests you carry this warrant because you're looking to collect the reward on me."

Sam had regained his feet. He shook his head, trying to clear the cobwebs.

Crawford backhanded him, hard. "Well?" he demanded.

Sam spit blood from his mouth. "What if I am?"

"So I was right not to tell you who I really was, when we were crossing the *Jornada*," Crawford said. "But I don't understand. You had other chances to kill me. Last night, for instance. There was nothing to stop you. Why didn't you do it?"

"I thought about it," Sam said. "I couldn't go through with it. I don't know why."

"And Quirt Evans—was it you who drowned

him in that stream?"

"Call it a swimming lesson."

"And it was also you who alerted the Apaches?"

"More or less," Sam said.

"Then you're responsible for our failure to kill Nanay—not to mention the deaths of many good men."

"I wouldn't exactly call them 'good,' " Sam told him. "I doubt there was a rush on the Pearly Gates when they died."

Around the front of the old mission church, the girlfriends and wives of the dead scalp hunters cried, "Kill him! Kill him, now!"

Crawford had become calm again. "I'm disappointed in you, my friend. Very disappointed. And, to think, I saved your life."

"That was your mistake," Sam said.

"On the contrary," said Crawford. "I think you will find that it was yours."

He crushed the warrant in his fist and let it fall to the ground. Then he turned. "What is your interest in Slater, Mr. Honeycutt?"

Honeycutt flashed a big, sloppy grin. He'd lowered his rifle some. "Simple. There's a reward on his head."

"A reward? For the West's most famous bounty hunter?"

Honeycutt chuckled. "Yeah. It's a hoot, ain't it? See, I'm a bounty hunter myself. I travel one end of the West to the other. As I go, I collect paper.

One day when I was up north, I came across an old, yellowed warrant for Sam Slater. I recognized the name—everybody in the law business has heard of The Regulator. Seems he's wanted for murder, in Montana. Reward's two thousand dollars. It was hard to believe, but I wired the authorities up there to see if the warrant was still good. And what do you know? It was. So I went after him. Hunting The Regulator. It's the ultimate game." He smiled that sloppy smile again. "I've trailed him a long ways. And I've won."

"A good piece of work," Crawford commented. "You must know the *Jornada*, to have survived after we shot your horse."

"I served out here with the 6th Cavalry, chasing Cochise. It was after my discharge that I took up bounty hunting. Pay's better, and it's more fun."

While they talked, Sam pretended to still be stunned from the blow with the rifle butt. He waited for his chance. He knew he would only get one.

To Honeycutt, Crawford said, "So you want us to let you have Slater?"

"That's right," Honeycutt said, lowering the rifle a bit more.

"There's a reward on my head, too," Crawford pointed out. "On the heads of all these men. How do we know you're not after that, as well?"

Honeycutt said, "I got no quarrel with you, Crawford. Slater's the one I want. I come more'n two thousand miles to get him, too. I get Slater, and I'll be the number-one bounty hunter. *I'll* be The Regulator. The best. That's worth more to me than any amount of money."

Crawford nodded, a glint of appreciation in his boyish eyes. At that moment, Sam threw himself at Honeycutt, going for his rifle. He knocked the rifle barrel down. The weapon went off, and the bullet went into the dirt. Sam tried to wrench the rifle out of Honeycutt's hands, but the big man spun him around and sent him skidding. Sam came back. Before Honeycutt could raise the rifle again, Sam threw a shoulder into his chest—and bounced off.

The big man grinned.

"Oh, shit," Sam said.

Honeycutt tossed the rifle to Crawford. "Come on, Slater."

The big man moved in, hamlike fists raised. Sam gave him a left to the stomach—it was like hitting a side of beef—then hit him with his best punch, an overhand right to the jaw.

Honeycutt shrugged it off. He hit Sam two clubbing blows to the head that knocked him backward.

Sam came on again. He ducked a swinging blow, reached up, and flicked off the big man's thick eyeglasses.

Honeycutt groped around, half blind. "You son-of-a-bitch . . ."

Sam stepped on the glasses, breaking them. Then he kicked Honeycutt in the shin. Honeycutt yelped and hopped on one leg. Sam rained blows on the big man's face. Honeycutt lunged forward and hung on, trying to clear his head. Sam tried to push off. Honeycutt hugged him tighter, crushing his ribs. Sam couldn't breathe. At last, Honeycutt let him go. Sam stood helplessly, sucking in air. He looked, saw what was coming, and grimaced. A right hand hit his cheek with the impact of a runaway train. The next thing Sam knew, he was on his back.

Sam looked up, seeing double. Honeycutt kicked him in the side of the head, laying him out. Sam had been kicked by horses that hadn't hurt that much.

The crowd was yelling. Out of the fog of pain, Sam saw Teresa looking at him anxiously. Then he saw Crawford. The scalp hunter had a little grin on his face. He shook his head, "Sam. Sam."

Honeycutt found his glasses and put them back on. Both lenses were cracked. Honeycutt growled with anger. He took his rifle back from Crawford and pointed it at Sam, ready to squeeze the trigger.

Crawford held out a hand, stopping him. "Wait. I know a better way, if you're open to it."

Honeycutt was breathing heavily. He looked curious. "I'm open to anything good. All I need is his head in one piece. I figure to pickle it and take it as evidence that I really killed him. Hell, I can exhibit it on the side and make me some extra money."

"Good," Crawford said. "Very enterprising. Then, if you'll allow us, we'll dispose of him in a more . . . shall we say, leisurely.fashion." He turned. "Sam, what happened? I trusted you. I *liked* you. Yet you betrayed me."

Sam said, "You make yourself sound like some kind of saint, Crawford. Cut the fancy talk, and let's get to the good part."

"Oh, it will be good, believe me," Crawford told him. "Tie his hands, Mr. Slocum."

While Werdann and Kingsley covered Sam with their rifles, Slocum tied Sam's hands behind his back.

Crawford started away. "Bring him along," he ordered.

CHAPTER 15

KINGSLEY AND WERDANN PRODDED SAM, none too gently, with their rifle barrels. He followed Crawford. Slocum walked beside him, glowering. "Sam Slater—The Regulator. Imagine that. I thought you was our friend. Hell, I even offered to help you."

"He won't be regulatin' nobody no more," chuckled the Texas gunman, Werdann.

The crowd of women and hangers-on followed them. Sam tried to look for Teresa, but Kingsley, the man with the wounded head, jabbed him with the rifle.

"Keep going, damn you. Because of you, all our friends is dead."

"And we're out the five thousand pesos we would have got for Nanay," Werdann added.

In front of Sam, Crawford turned to Honeycutt, the huge bounty hunter. "You're our guest, Mr. Honeycutt. You may choose the means of Mr. Slater's demise. We only have until tomorrow morning, because we must vacate these premises, so some of the more sophisticated options are not open to us."

"As long as I get his head," Honeycutt reminded, "in good enough shape that he can be identified."

"You shall. You shall. Tell me, what sounds better—shall we roast him over a fire, or stake him out on an anthill?"

The bounty hunter stumbled over an empty bottle. He couldn't see very well with his cracked glasses. It was incongruous, a man so big and powerful, with such weak eyes. He said, "I seen fellas roasted alive once, by Comanches, over to Texas. Never seen a man staked on an anthill, though. Pretty good, is it?"

"You'll love it," Crawford assured him. "Kingsley, fetch a jug of molasses, will you?"

The usually sullen Kingsley grinned and hurried back to the mission.

The scalp hunters led Sam through the gate and off the promontory. Sam's head throbbed where he'd been hit by the rifle butt, but that was the least of his worries right now. He'd seen men staked out on anthills. He knew what he was in for. He knew that, in the end, he'd be reduced to a quivering, screaming mass, begging to die, as the ants ate him alive.

The little procession made its way to a spot near the bottom of the hill. Sam figured he'd rather be gunned down than killed by ants. Suddenly he broke away, running for the river. With luck, one clean shot would take him out. And, who knew, there was always a chance he'd get away. It would be dark soon. If he could just . . .

There was a rifle shot, and a bullet whined by his ear.

"Don't shoot!" he heard Crawford cry. "Can't you see, that's what he wants."

It was hard running with his hands tied behind him. Sam stumbled over a dip in the earth. He heard footsteps behind him. They drew closer. Sam pumped his long legs as hard as he could, but he couldn't outrun them like this. Then somebody tackled him, sending him sprawling face first to the rocky ground.

He lay there, spitting dirt from his mouth. He tried to get up, but before he could, a noose was dropped around his neck.

"Drag him along," Crawford said.

Slocum and Werdann pulled on the rope. Sam lurched to his feet to avoid being choked. The two scalp hunters hauled him along, his Apache moccasins scrabbling against the rocky ground. He couldn't tell where they were headed. All he could see was the ground. At last they stopped. Strong hands grabbed Sam by the collar and threw him to the ground.

The breath was knocked from him. After a second, he rolled over. His face was scratched and full of gravel. His mouth was bleeding again. He tried to shake the cobwebs out of his head, to think of a plan of action. But before he could do anything, his feet were grabbed, tied, and secured to the ground with wooden stakes, pounded in with pistol butts.

"There," said Slocum, standing above him. "That'll slow you down a bit."

Sam twisted his head and looked around. To his left were a series of turned-up anthills. Red ants ran all over them. Sam's blood froze. Already some of the ants scouted over his shirt sleeve. Something nipped his wrist.

Honeycutt chuckled. "Damn! This is going to be some good."

The women crowded around, yelling for Sam's blood, wanting revenge for their dead husbands and lovers. Sam couldn't smell the tequila on their breaths but he could see it in their contorted faces. He pulled against the stakes that held his feet, but they had been driven in too tightly. The scalp hunters laughed at his futile efforts.

Slocum and Werdann ripped off Sam's shirt, cutting it because his hands were tied. "The pants, too?" Kingsley said.

"Heavens, no," laughed Crawford. "There are ladies present."

Already ants were running over Sam's naked chest and stomach. He felt their tiny, powerful jaws biting him. A few bites would hurt. They would raise red lumps on his skin. Thousands on thousands of bites would strip the flesh from his bones. He had seen it happen.

Kingsley was back, and Crawford said, "Mr. Kingsley. If you'll apply the molasses, please."

Kingsley grinned. He tipped the molasses jug and poured the sticky liquid, using his hand to spread the molasses over Sam's exposed chest, neck, and back.

"Remember, leave the head," Honeycutt cautioned.

Kingsley was done. Swearing, he shook off as many as he could of the ants that were now crawling all over his hands and forearms, then he scrubbed off the rest with dirt. Crawford motioned, and Slocum cut the rope that bound Sam's hands. He and Werdann each grabbed one of Sam's arms. Sam fought violently, but with his feet pinned, he had no chance. The two scalp hunters dragged his upper body around and dropped it across the anthills. They stretched his arms to their limits, tied ropes around each wrist, and bound them to stakes driven into the ground.

Sam looked up. The light was fading. There were already torches in the crowd. Some of the women squatted, getting ready to enjoy the show. They had tequila and tortillas, and blankets to wrap around themselves. They were preparing to spend the night, to watch the whole thing. Sam looked around, but he didn't see Teresa.

The red ants boiled out of their mounds, disturbed by this huge alien presence, attracted by the sweet molasses. The ants swarmed over Sam's chest and neck. They got into his trousers, into his hair. He closed his eyes. *Please, God,* he thought, *don't let them get in my eyes.* In no time, he was covered with ants. He felt like he was on fire. He struggled against his bonds, trying to shake them off. It was no good. He was held tight.

More ants came, uncounted numbers of them. Their jaws dug into Sam like thousands of fiery needle pricks. Around him, he heard yelling and laughing. He opened his eyes again. The night sky seemed to be spinning, and in its vortex, he saw Crawford and Honeycutt. He fixed his vision on the bounty hunter's long blond pigtail. He tried to concentrate, to ignore the pain that was boring inside him. The ants were devouring his skin, next they would work their way inside, to his muscles and vital organs. It would take them a while, though, a long while.

Sam had no idea how much time had passed. *Concentrate,* he told himself. *Concentrate. Ignore the pain. Look at Honeycutt's pigtail. Try to count the twists in the braid.* He heard Crawford laughing. The laughter seemed to come from far away. The blond pigtail swam in his vision. It moved, alive, like a snake. Nearby, someone was screaming, and Sam realized that it was him. The

Apaches had taught him to endure pain, but he had never felt anything like this. His Apache father, Loco, would have been disappointed. Sam could see the old man's reproving face in front of him, but he didn't care. He screamed. He cried out. He fought the ropes that held him down. *Father, I'm sorry. I'm not worthy. I'm sorry.*

Above his screams, he heard something else. Gunshots. Then more of them.

"Apaches!" someone cried. "The Apaches have come! Get back to the mission!"

There was a great upheaval around Sam. People struggled to their feet. They dropped bottles of tequila and ran for the safety of the promontory and the mission. More shots sounded.

"Hurry!" Crawford cried. "Get back before they cut us off!"

The bounty hunter, Honeycutt, pointed to Sam. "What about him?"

"He's not going anywhere," Crawford told him. "Come on."

The two men followed the others to the mission. As they did, Honeycutt turned and snapped a rifle shot at Sam, anyway, with his Smith & Wesson; but because of his cracked eyeglasses the bullet missed, grazing Sam's rib and digging itself into the earth.

The scalp hunters and their women retreated up the hill. Then, out of the darkness, a deeper shadow appeared. The shadow knelt beside Sam. It was a woman.

"Teresa," he groaned.

"Yes." She scooped dirt over his chest and neck, more and more of it, smothering as many of the ants as she could, momentarily lessening the pain. She sawed his bonds with a knife.

"You fired those shots," Sam said.

"Yes. Now, get away, while you can. Go upstream and hide."

Sam sat up, half delirious, rubbing the circulation back into his wrists and legs. The ants were still all over him, imprisoned by the molasses, still biting him. He tried to brush away the sticky mess. It did no good. He felt like he was on fire.

"Come . . .come with me," he croaked to Teresa.

"No," she said.

"But Crawford. He'll . . ."

"No he won't. In his way, Thomas cares for me. I'll be all right." She hesitated, and her voice lowered. "Anyway, you . . .you do not really want me. I realize that. I would just be in your way."

Sam said, "Teresa, I—"

She put a finger to his lips, cutting him off. "No. Now, go. Quickly. Please."

She helped him to his feet. He tried to brush away the ants again, then gave up. The pain was so great that he couldn't think. He felt like he was going mad.

"Go," she said again, and she gave him a little push. Then she was gone herself, hurrying toward the promontory.

From the mission, there were rifle shots. Some fool up there had gotten jumpy and opened fire at nothing. All the more luck for Sam. He stumbled along. He hoped he was headed for the river. He didn't know how long he had been walking. He didn't even know if he was going in a straight line. Pain consumed him. Several times he fell to the ground and rolled in the dirt like a dog or a bear, trying to scrape off the ants. Then he got back up again and kept going.

At last his moccasined feet splashed water. The river. He cried with relief. He waded to the middle of the stream. He let the cold water come up his body, over his waist, over his chest, up to his neck. He felt the pain recede. Then the ants were climbing for safety, thousands of them, up his neck and jaws, into his nose, his hair. He let himself slip under water. He stayed down as long as he could. He got up, took a deep breath and went under again, washing the ants from his body and out of his hair. He stayed down until he thought his lungs would explode, then he raised his head. He went under one more time, then he dragged himself to the far side of the stream. Thank God it wasn't deep; he couldn't have swum.

He reached the far shore. He lay there and took a drink. Then he crept along the shore, digging up mud. He packed the mud onto his chest and ribs and as much of his back as he could reach. He packed it around his neck, over his face and in his hair, to soothe the pain. Then he crawled downstream as far as he could go. It wasn't as far as he would have liked, but it couldn't be helped. If the scalp hunters searched for him tomorrow, they were bound to find him. He had to hope they rode out at first light, like Crawford had planned.

He found a stand of brush. He pushed himself into its cover, heedless of the thorns that scratched him, and he fell asleep. His sleep was broken by waves of pain, and in his tormented dreams he heard screaming.

CHAPTER 16

SAM CAME TO. FLIES BUZZED DULLY IN HIS mud-caked ears. He could tell by the light that filtered through the brush that it was midday. What had seemed like good cover last night was hardly anything at all when viewed by day. He would have been plainly visible to anyone riding by. The scalp hunters must not have looked for him. They must have deserted their base at first light, as they had planned to do, scared of Nanay and his Apaches.

Sam tried to get up. Waves of pain and nausea forced him back down. His neck was stiff from being dragged by the rope and it was hard to move his head. He remembered the anthills, the feeling as the tiny creatures swarmed over him, devouring him. The mud on his body had dried stiff and heavy, like a plaster cast. Beneath it, his skin was raw and excruciatingly painful.

He had a burning thirst. He heard water gurgling, and he knew that he must be near the stream. Slowly, painfully, he rolled onto his stomach. He lay there a second, catching his breath, while the waves of pain receded. He dragged himself forward, thorns cutting his skin in the places it was not protected by the mud, and he stuck his head from the brush.

He watched and listened. There seemed to be no one about. Birds were singing. Across the stream, about a half-mile distant, he saw vultures swooping low behind a dip in the hill. They were probably feeding on a dead horse or mule, abandoned by the scalp hunters in their flight.

Sam crawled to the stream, pulling himself along, still watchful, trying to ignore the pain that consumed him. Even his teeth hurt. He was out of breath and sweating under the mud pack when he reached the water. He lay and drank.

He could see the promontory clearly from here. It looked quiet. The cornfields and cattle in the little valley were unattended, more evidence that Crawford and his scalp hunters had pulled out.

Should he try to catch them? He didn't know. He had no horse, no weapons. He hated to let Crawford do this to him and get away with it, but maybe he should leave well enough alone, and be thankful that he was still alive. It was only because of Teresa that he *was* alive. He hoped she was all right.

He drank some more. The water revived him. He realized that he was famished. If he had the time, he could make a bow and arrows. He could kill one of the steers that grazed in the valley. But there was no time. The Apaches might appear at any moment, and when they did, they weren't likely to be in a good mood.

The best place to find food would be on the promontory. Surely, in their flight, the scalp hunters and their camp followers had left something behind. He might find weapons up there, maybe even a horse.

When Sam had finished drinking, he stripped off his trousers and moccasins, and he bathed himself in the river, washing the mud from his skin and hair. His skin was red and raw; it oozed blood from the attacks of the ants. Exposure to the air was painful, and the slightest movement made it worse. Sam grit his teeth. Tears flowed down his scarred cheek. He covered his chest, arms, and neck with a thinner layer of mud. The mud would take the edge off the pain, and it would cool him against the heat.

Slowly, he put his pants and moccasins back on. He crossed the stream. He was still watchful, but there was no movement, no sign of human life. He seemed to be alone in the valley. What if he was wrong, though? What if some of the scalp hunters were still up there, watching him even now? Common sense told him that was not likely, however, not with Nanay on their trail.

Leaving the stream, Sam crossed the ground that he had traversed the night before. It all seemed different. He felt pain with each step. Now and then the delirium of last night threatened to return, and he had to stop. He was weak, and breath came with difficulty.

He started up the hill toward the promontory. Ahead, he saw the vultures. Then he topped the little rise in the hill, and he stopped.

In front of him was a body, or something that had once been a body, because most of it was now bones and raw meat. It was staked out on the row of anthills, where Sam himself had been. What the ants had missed, vultures now picked through.

Sam stumbled forward, yelling, throwing rocks at the great birds. "Get away! Go!"

The vultures flapped their long wings, reluctant to leave their feed. "Go! God damn it, go!" Sam cried, hurling rocks wildly at them, unable to aim because of tear-filled eyes. At last, the vultures lifted slowly and awkwardly from the ground. They circled overhead as Sam ran forward to the body.

"Oh, God," he said.

It was Teresa, or what was left of her. Sam fell to his knees and hung his head.

Crawford had staked Teresa to the anthills for

saving Sam's life. The screams that Sam had heard last night had been no dream. They had been Teresa's. A hole in the girl's skull showed that, before the ants had finished their work, somebody had mercifully put an end to her agony. In his deep sleep, Sam hadn't heard the shot.

Sam turned away. Teresa had loved him, or thought that she did. She'd been with these depraved scalp hunters for so long that a man like Sam had seemed virtuous to her. She had thought she'd seen good qualities in him, qualities she had only imagined. She had realized that he had no feelings for her, though; so rather than be a burden, she had not come with him. She had trusted in Crawford's affection for her. That trust had cost her life.

Sam knew then that he was going after Crawford and his men. He was going to catch them, however long it took, whatever obstacles he might have to overcome. And when he caught them, he was going to kill them. Not for the reward, but for the pleasure of it.

He cut Teresa's body—it wasn't really a body, any more—free. He carried it into the shade and piled heavy rocks on top of the remains. He couldn't do anything about the ants, but he could at least keep the birds and wild animals off what was left of her. There was no time for anything more elaborate. He would have said a prayer, but he was not a praying man.

Revenge was more his style.

He started back to the promontory, moving warily, from cover to cover where there was any. He came across fresh tracks, where the scalp hunters had departed that morning. Not far from where he had buried Teresa, the tracks split. A large group of horses and mules had gone downstream, toward Mexico. That looked to be the women and the few men who serviced the scalp hunters on the promontory—the cantina owner, and some others. Four sets of prints broke off from the main body. They crossed the stream, heading toward the *Jornada* and the States. Sam recognized Crawford's horse among them.

There was one set of prints that Sam didn't see—those of Honeycutt, the huge bounty hunter. Sam backtracked, but he found nothing. A man that size, his prints would be impossible to miss. He hadn't gone with the women, or with Crawford.

Which meant what? Had Honeycutt been killed by Crawford and the scalp hunters? That was possible. They didn't trust Honeycutt. For all Honeycutt's talk about wanting to become *The* Regulator, Crawford and his men were worth a lot more money dead than Sam was, and money was one hell of a motivator. Sam should know.

So Honeycutt was dead, or else he was out there somewhere, looking for Sam, willing to chance being caught by the Apaches, in return for Sam's head.

Sam reached the causeway that leads onto

the promontory. He waited a while, watching. The old mission seemed quiet. Even at this distance, Sam could see evidence of the scalp hunters' hasty departure. Lying in the brush, he was so weak and hungry that he almost fell asleep. He fought the urge to give in to his weariness and pain. He pushed himself to keep going.

He got to his feet and crossed the causeway. The rock fell away steeply on either side of him. He passed through the mission gate and across the yard. He passed the church. The ground was littered with discarded articles of clothing, with bottles and old carpet bags. Even the chickens and goats were gone.

Beyond the church, Sam came to a string of adobe and brush *jacales*. The adobe buildings looked slightly more substantial than the *jacales*, so he decided to try them first. He approached the first one, pushed aside the cowhide that served as a door, and stepped inside.

It was dark in here, and cool. On a crude table in the center of the front room was a stack of tortillas. *Jackpot*, he thought. He crammed the tortillas in his mouth; he'd never imagined tortillas could taste so good. There was an *olla*, a clay water jug, nearby. Sam unstopped it and smelled. Mescal. His stomach turned, and he tossed the jug across the room. Another *olla* contained water, and he used it to wash down the tortillas. He searched the house for more substantial food, but there was nothing. There were no weapons either, save for a *cuchillo*, a long, thin-bladed Mexican knife, that Sam stuck in his belt.

Sam pushed aside the rawhide flap, starting for the next house. As he did, there was a shot, and a bullet plowed into the adobe next to his head.

CHAPTER 17

SAM DROPPED BACK INSIDE THE ADOBE house, breathing hard. A second shot chipped the doorjamb, spraying him with adobe.

It was dark in here, with the cowhide filling the door and the small rear window closed. "You had ten minutes to set up that shot, Honeycutt," Sam called out. "Is that the best you can do?"

The pigtailed bounty hunter was in the doorway of the house opposite. His gruff voice called back, "You son-of-a-bitch, Slater. If you hadn't broke my glasses, I'd of put that bullet between your goddamn eyes."

Sam sat with his back to the wall. "Don't you carry an extra pair?"

"They got broke when you shot my horse from under me."

Sam had to laugh. The laughter made his entire body ache. He felt fresh blood oozing beneath the layer of mud with which he'd covered himself. Honeycutt must have stalked him across the mission yard, yet Sam hadn't been aware of him. He had to admit that Honeycutt was good. The big man must be unsure whether or not Sam had a gun. That's why he didn't come right after him.

"How come you waited for me here?" Sam yelled out.

"I figured you had to come back," Honeycutt said. "Why go looking for you and maybe miss you, or even walk into some kind of trap?"

"You're either clever or lazy, Honeycutt. I ain't figured out which."

That got Honeycutt mad. He said, "Figure this out, you bastard." He started toward the adobe house.

There was no back way out. Sam's only hope was Honeycutt's bad eyes. Sam gathered himself. He thrust aside the cowhide, dashed out the door, and dived across the ground, rolling. Honeycutt snapped a shot at him but missed.

Sam came to his feet. The dive and roll had torn open his ravaged upper body. The pain almost took his breath away. He got his legs under him and ran around the side of the house as another bullet thwacked into the adobe behind him.

Honeycutt swore and came after him. Sam moved behind the house, putting another wall between himself and the bounty hunter's rifle. He had to outrun Honeycutt. He had to get off the promontory and into the mountains, where he could hide.

He moved to the rear of the next house and stopped, catching his breath. His body wanted to quit, but he had to keep going. He wondered if Honeycutt had gotten a fresh horse from the scalp hunters, and if he had, where it was.

Behind him, there was no sound. Honeycutt had stopped again, waiting for Sam to make the next move.

Looking around, Sam saw that he had moved in the opposite direction from the mission gate. He was farther from leaving the promontory than ever. He could climb down the promontory's steep rock sides, but it would be a slow climb, and he would be a hell of a target that way—even for somebody with bad eyes, like Honeycutt. A climb like that would take time, too. If Honeycutt had a horse, he could ride around and wait for Sam at the bottom. Sam had no weapon to fight the bounty hunter, except the *cuchillo* he'd found in the house. He couldn't match Honeycutt physically—he'd already learned that.

He would have to try to work his way along these houses, past the stables, past the church, and out the gate. Maybe he could catch Honeycutt looking the other way.

Where *was* Honeycutt, anyway? The big bastard was silent as a cat. It was hard to believe. Sam's senses were alive. He smelled Honeycutt. The bounty hunter was close, but that was all Sam knew.

Sam wiped sweat from his eyes. His body was in agony after diving along the rocky ground, but he had to put the pain out of his mind. Before him was a little warren of adobe houses and brush *jacales*. Sam drew in his breath. He set himself. He ran to his left. He turned down the side of a *jacale*.

And found Honeycutt right in front of him.

Sam threw himself to the ground as Honeycutt's rifle went off. Sam heard the bullet whine overhead. He got up and scrambled back around the side of the *jacale*. He ran down the narrow lane for all he was worth, turned right, and headed for the stables. Honeycutt's footsteps were right behind him. On top of everything else, Honeycutt was fast. The rifle fired again. Splinters flew from a *jacale's* brush wall.

Sam broke into the open, running past what had once been the mission granary. He stumbled in an old wagon rut, fell to one hand, got up, and kept going. He saw the mission gate in the distance, but he didn't have the strength left to get there. In his condition he couldn't outrun Honeycutt, anyway. He dodged right, in front of the old mission church. He ducked inside the carved church doorway, sprawling in the dirt and trash on the flagstone floor.

He got up. It was gloomy inside the church. Sunbeams filtered through the windows and the partly collapsed roof. In front of him were the dusty, littered altar and the wooden reredos, or screen, behind it. The faded native frescoes stared down from the walls. Sam shivered. The place seemed full of ghosts. Tethered to a stone candleholder in the far wall was a horse—Honeycutt's.

Behind Sam, it was quiet again. Honeycutt must be waiting to see if Sam tried to sneak through the church and out the back door that led from the sacristy. Sam looked around. He padded through the narrow door that led to the bell tower.

The tower's cupola roof was still intact. Light came through the windows just below it. A wooden landing ran around the bell floor. The two floors in between had collapsed or been cannibalized for their wood, but Sam saw handholds chiseled into the tower's walls.

He began to climb.

He moved as fast as he could. He would hide in the shadows on the bell floor. With luck, Honeycutt would think he had somehow gotten out of the church unnoticed. He would go looking for Sam off the promontory. By the time he realized his mistake and came back, Sam would be long gone.

Sam reached the bell floor. The ancient boards creaked as he tested their weight. He stepped into what looked like the darkest corner. The floor collapsed beneath him. He jumped back, crouching against the fieldstone wall as the broken floorboards fell the length of the tower to the well below, where they landed with a crash. Honeycutt was bound to hear that.

Sam looked around. An old ladder was propped against the wall. It just reached the crossbeam which supported the bronze bell. That gave Sam an idea.

He began climbing the ladder. He didn't have much time. Near the top, one of the ancient rungs gave way beneath his feet. He slipped and almost fell off. Then he steadied himself, pulled himself up to the next rung, and began to climb again.

He reached the heavy crossbeam. He swung onto it, his injured body groaning with pain. He crawled along the crossbeam, praying that the beam would hold his weight, along with the weight of the hundred-pound bell. If it didn't, it was a long drop.

He got to the bell. The bronze had turned green from age and lack of polishing. There were three loops at the bell's top—representing the Trinity, Sam supposed. Heavy chains had been passed through each of these loops, then bolted around the crossbeam. As Sam had hoped, the iron chains were rusted through. Sam drew the *cuchillo* from his belt. He worked the knife blade into the bolt closure. The rusted metal flaked away. Sam dug at the metal. More fell away. He kept digging, sawing through the rust. Then he was through. The chain was broken. Noiselessly, he drew the chain from the bronze loop and hung it over the crossbeam. He began to work on the next chain.

Below, he heard Honeycutt enter the church. The big bounty hunter must have heard the floorboards falling. He must know that Sam had not tried to get out the back way. Sam heard faint footfalls on the stone floor.

"Slater?" It was Honeycutt's voice.

Sam kept cutting through the second chain. Sweat poured into his eyes. He wiped them on his shoulder. Waves of pain swept over him until he thought he would faint, but he fought through them.

The footsteps withdrew to the far end of the church, toward the wooden reredos.

There. Sam broke the second chain. He withdrew it from the bell's loop and frantically started work on the last, center chain.

The footsteps were coming closer again.

Sam was almost through the chain's bolt. Putting the *cuchillo* aside, he lay on the crossbeam and took the hundred-pound bell's other two loops in his hands. Gently, he let the bell down, until its weight snapped what was left of the bolt. The chain slipped noiselessly onto the top of the bell.

"Slater?" Honeycutt was approaching the bell tower.

"In here," Sam said, grimacing. The veins on his arms and neck stood out as he lay astride the crossbeam, holding the great bell.

Honey cutt's tone was confident. "You're hit, ain't you?"

"Yeah." Sam didn't have to fake the strain in his voice. His arm and shoulder muscles were shaking.

Far below, Honeycutt's bulk filled the ill-lit tower well. The bounty hunter was puzzled, as he looked around. "Where the hell are you?"

Sam let go of the heavy bell. He watched it fall through space. "Here," he said.

Honeycutt looked up. For a second, the expression on his myopic face froze. Then the bell hit his head with a crunch and a doleful gong.

CHAPTER 18

SAM SWUNG OFF THE CROSSBEAM, ONTO the ladder. He climbed slowly down the bell tower. Honeycutt was dead, but there had never been any doubt about that. The pigtailed bounty hunter's skull had been crushed by the falling bell. Blood and some kind of gray liquid spilled across the stone floor.

Sam took the dead man's rifle, pistol, and shell belt. With an effort, he removed Honeycutt's shirt from the heavy body, trying not to look at the bounty hunter's mangled head. He put on the shirt himself, for protection from the sun. The shirt was huge on him, so he sliced off the sleeves with his *cuchillo.*

He stumbled outside the bell tower, crossing the mission yard to the well. He winched up the bucket and drank. He splashed water on his face. He was tired and feverish. He would have given anything to lay down and sleep, but that option was not open to him. The Apaches could come at any time, and Crawford and his men already had at least an eight-hour start on him.

He went back inside the church, where he searched Honeycutt's saddlebags. He found plug tobacco, jerky, and tortillas—Honeycutt's provisions for crossing the *Jornada.* There were four canteens full of water, plus grain for the horse. Sam rolled a piece of the jerky in one of the tortillas and wolfed it down. He threw away things like the tobacco that he would not need, then he saddled and bridled the bounty hunter's big gray gelding.

He mounted and rode away from the mission. The horse was adequate at best. It had bottom, but not much speed. With its size, it would use up a lot of water and grain. It was not the mount that Sam would have picked to catch Crawford in the *Jornada.* Actually, a mule would have been best. The gray gelding would have to do, though.

Sam rode down from the hills, into the little valley. Near the stream, he paused. With Honeycutt's rifle, he shot one of the scalp hunters' abandoned steers. He cut out the animal's liver and ate the salty organ raw, a delicacy to which he'd become accustomed in his days with the Apaches. He cut strips of meat for later. But he hadn't killed the steer primarily for food. He emptied the animal's intestine. He tied the intestine at one end with a strip of rawhide. He filled it with water from the stream, then tied off the other end. He made a rope sling and hung the water-filled intestine from his saddle horn, to go with Honeycutt's canteens.

He rode on, following the scalp hunters' trail. They were leaving by the same route that Sam and Crawford had come. They would probably cross the *Jornada* by the same route, as well. Sam picked up his pace, pausing only now and then to be sure he was still on their trail. He climbed high into the Eagle Mountains, into the land of pines and crisp air.

That night, he camped among the pines. It was cold, but he dared not risk a fire. He was used to freezing nights like this, without fire, from days spent roaming the mountains with the Apaches, hiding from American and Mexican soldiers. He ate some of the beef strips that he had cut that afternoon, along with Honeycutt's tortillas. He grained the big gray gelding and set him to graze.

Sam slept fitfully that night. There was too much pain in his body for him to be comfortable. The next day, he was off well before dawn. Early that morning, he crossed the divide and began his descent from the mountains. Before noon, he was on the *Jornada del Fuego*. He figured he'd made up an hour and a half on the fleeing scalp hunters. Their tracks were easy enough to read. Along with Crawford, there were three others in the group—Slocum, Kingsley, and Werdann, most likely.

Sam pushed the gray gelding hard. He still had six and a half hours to make up. Once again, he fought the spell of the *Jornada*, where time seemed to stand still under the relentless onslaught of the sun. He had to urge both himself and the gelding on. He was still feverish from being staked out on the anthills. He drifted in and out of consciousness, awakening once with a start, to find that his horse had stopped. He looked at the sun. Nearly an hour had passed. He swore and kicked the horse's ribs savagely. He would have to be in better shape than this when he caught up with Crawford and his scalp hunters.

Then he remembered Teresa. He remembered what she had looked like when the scalp hunters were done with her. He remembered the Apaches that he had seen slaughtered in the Sierra Negros, and the family of sheepherders. The fog seemed to lift from his brain, and he recovered his grim sense of purpose.

He rode through the noon heat, sparing neither himself nor his animal. This leg of the journey was different from the one he'd made with Crawford, due to the detour they'd taken in pursuit of Nanay. He was not sure where the next water was, so he had to stop at sunset. He didn't want to lose the scalp hunters' tracks.

He was off again as soon as it was light enough to read sign. At about eight that morning, he came to the little *tinaja* where Crawford and his men had stopped yesterday evening. The *tinaja* was high in the hills, and there was damn little water left in it. The signs showed that the scalp hunters had not stayed here, however. There had still been daylight left, so they had ridden on after watering themselves and their animals. Sam topped off his canteens and the steer's intestine with the scummy water, and he followed. About two hours later, he came to the place where the scalp hunters had camped. They had made a cold camp, too. They were fearful of pursuit by Nanay and the Apaches. Sam found an empty whiskey bottle at the camp.

He picked the bottle up. "So Crawford still has trouble sleeping," he said aloud. He tossed the bottle away. "He should."

Sam remembered this country now. He was confident Crawford and his men would make for the box-canyon seep spring next. He knew the way there. With only the briefest of rests, he traveled the rest of the day and long into the night, guiding himself by the stars. Tomorrow night, the scalp hunters would seek water at the *tinaja* called Dead Man's Tanks.

Sam intended to give that name new meaning.

It was well before sunup the next day when Sam broke camp. The gray gelding was holding up better than Sam had expected. The horse had done everything Sam had asked of it, however reluctantly. Then, in the predawn darkness, the big gray misfooted in a shallow ravine and came up lame.

Sam dismounted. The gray was holding up its right foreleg. Even in the dark, a cursory examination with his hands told Sam that the leg was broken. Sam was alone on the desert, without a horse.

Sam killed the horse, slitting its throat with the *cuchillo.* He could not chance a gunshot. He took the jerky and some of the tortillas from the saddlebag and put them in his shirt. He drew the Smith & Wesson hunting rifle from its scabbard. He crammed his shirt and trouser pockets with bullets. He tied his pistol holster down so it would not slap against his leg. He filled the steer's intestine with water from the canteens, then he drank the rest of the water in the canteens and threw them away. He slung the intestine over his shoulder. Lastly, he tied his bandana around his head, Apache style, to keep the hair and sweat out of his eyes.

Then he took the rifle in his right hand, and he began to run.

CHAPTER 19

SAM FOLLOWED THE SCALP HUNTERS' TRACKS.

An Apache could travel faster on foot than a white man could on horseback. Sam remembered his Apache foster father, Loco, taking him on long training runs in the mountains, to build up his wind and legs. Sam had been proud of his ability to run. He had prided himself on being as good as any Apache. But it had been a long time since those training runs, and Loco hadn't staked him on an anthill first.

It took a while for Sam to get his legs under him. He wasn't used to this anymore. His breath came hard. The sweat made the wounds on his body burn. In addition, all the water he'd drunk before he had started lay heavy in his stomach. That was all right—he'd use up that water, and more, before he was through.

Gradually, his breathing became more regular. His legs stopped feeling like blocks of wood. They grew stronger, more supple. He began to get a rhythm. His body began to feel like a well-oiled machine, operating smoothly and efficiently. He jogged along, taking short steps, with no wasted motion of hands or head. When the rifle grew heavy, he switched it to his other hand. Now and then, he stopped for a sip from the intestine full of water, then kept going.

The sun rose higher. The fierce heat beat down. The sweat dried as it came out of Sam's body, leaving only the salt to burn his wounds. Once again, he passed the detritus of westward expansion—the wagons, graves, abandoned furniture and equipment. The country was rugged, ridge after ridge of barren, rocky hills, whose mineral content made them look purple when seen from a distance. There were no trees, no mesquite, no cactus. Here and there a forlorn clump of creosote stood out, the only living things on this sun-baked eternity of sand and rock.

Hell must look something like this, Sam thought.

The rocks absorbed the sun's heat and reflected it back in shimmering waves. It was like running in an oven, but Sam kept on, through the morning and into the afternoon. He was gaining on the scalp hunters. He could tell from their tracks. He was not far behind them now.

He had to plan what to do when he caught them. Ideally, he would get to Dead Man's Tanks before they did. If he controlled the water, he could force them to come to him. They'd have no choice, if they didn't want to die of thirst. It would be hard to get to the Tanks first, though, since he would have to make a long detour to avoid being seen. His other choice was to let the scalp hunters get there first and make camp. He could hit them late at night. With luck, he'd catch Crawford drunk, if not all of them. Or, he could attack them at dawn and hope that Crawford was too hungover to put up much resistance.

It was midafternoon. The harsh shadows were beginning to lengthen. Sam topped another long, rock-strewn ridge. Then he stopped. Something was moving in the distance. It was a rider.

Sam crouched low on the skyline, shading his eyes with a hand. The rider was one of the scalp hunters; Sam couldn't recognize him at this range. The man had straggled behind the others. Maybe he'd had problems with his horse, or maybe the scalp hunters were losing discipline in their flight—though that was hard to believe with Crawford in charge.

Sam examined the landscape. He didn't want any shooting, if possible. He looked for a place where he could intercept the rider. The man was following a natural trail through the rocky country. Farther ahead, Sam saw a narrow pass. If the man kept his present course—as he was almost bound to do—he would have to go that way.

Sam dropped back below the ridge and ran to his right. He would circle around the rider, get ahead of him, and cut him off. He moved easily along the uneven ground, hopping from rock to rock where he had to. His blood lust was up, and all the pain he had endured seemed to fall away.

He got far out to the right, then turned and began to run parallel to the rider, keeping a long, irregular ridge between them. A lizard skittered out of his way.

The man had not been riding fast. When Sam thought he was well in front of him, he moved cautiously to the top of the ridge to check. He lay among the rocks of the ridge line, blending in, ignoring their red-hot surfaces as best he could. He saw the rider. The man was a good mile behind, coming on at a slow walk, every now and then looking behind him. Sam looked in the other direction. There was no sign of the other scalp hunters.

Sam moved on, to the spot where the trail narrowed. He hastened down from the ridge. The pass took a bend just before this, so he was in no danger of being seen by the rider. When he reached the valley floor, he took off his shirt and tied it around his waist, as an Apache did when preparing for battle. He hid his rifle, shell belt, food, and water skin in the rocks. He wouldn't be needing them. He rubbed dirt in his hair. He rubbed dirt over his body, wincing with the pain that action caused. He rubbed dirt into his trousers. Then he drew the long Mexican *cuchillo* from his belt. He laid beside the trail, and he threw more dirt over himself, until he was completely covered. He grasped the *cuchillo* in his right hand.

He lay motionless, under the beating sun. He stared straight ahead, willing himself to become a part of the landscape, the way Loco had taught him, long ago.

He smelled the horse and the man, smelled their rank sweat. Then he heard the steady *clop-clop* of hoofs.

Closer they came. Sam did not move, not even his eyes. The rider would suspect nothing. If he was looking anywhere for trouble, it would be up in the rocks.

Closer. Sam's hand tightened on the *cuchillo's* wooden grip. He gathered his muscles beneath him, ready to spring.

Closer. Man and horse were alongside him now, not five feet away.

Sam jumped from the ground. A bounding step took him to the horse, and he leaped with the knife poised. He saw that the rider was Kingsley—he recognized him from the bandage around his head—even as he tackled him and drove the point of the knife into his throat.

Both men toppled off the horse's opposite

side, landing in the dirt. Before Kingsley had time to react, Sam slit his throat. The scalp hunter scrabbled on his back, like a dying roach. He grasped at his throat, with the blood pouring out of him and the life fading from his eyes. He never even knew what had happened to him. Then his legs kicked out once, and he was still.

Kingsley's frightened horse had run off down the trail. *Let him go,* Sam thought. He was doing better without a horse. Maybe the Apaches would catch the poor beast before the coyotes did—though it was hard to say which group would treat the animal worse.

Sam wiped the bloody knife blade on his pants leg. He looked at the dead scalp hunter. For a moment he felt sorry for Kingsley. Then he remembered how Kingsley had shotgunned the Apache child during the attack on the village. He remembered how Kingsley had laughed when he'd spread the molasses over Sam's chest, by the anthills.

Sam's expression hardened. His only regret was that the bastard never knew who did this to him.

Sam got his water skin and took a drink. He buckled on his shell belt. He picked up his rifle and started running again.

CHAPTER 20

SLOCUM AND WERDANN STOOD NEXT TO their horses. The blazing afternoon sun beat down on them. There was no shade on the vast expanse of the *Jornada*. Werdann held the reins of Crawford's mount, as well as his own. Above them, Crawford stood at the crest of a ridge, looking over their back trail. Slocum and Werdann were hot and tired. They were low on water, and it showed in their dusty, sunburned faces. The gaunted horses hung their heads low, as if in submission to the relentless assault of the sun.

"Christ, I hate this country," Slocum said. The sun had dried the grease from his face, leaving only the dirt. It seemed to have melted his jowls, which hung limply.

Werdann, the rawhide-lean Texan, agreed. "When I get out of here, I want to go someplace it rains, or snows, even. I almost wish we'd took our chances and gone back through the mountains to Hermosilio. Least that way if we died, we'd have been looking at something green. There ain't nothin' out here but rocks. There ain't nothin' *alive*."

There was a little shower of stones, as Crawford descended the ridge. There was a worried look on Crawford's boyish face. He blinked his eyes against the sun's harsh glare and the headache that last night's bottle of whiskey had given him. It seemed like he always had a headache, anymore.

Slocum said, "You see Kingsley, Colonel?"

Crawford shook his head. "No. No sign of him. And you can see damn far from up there."

Slocum and Werdann exchanged glances. "Kingsley wasn't that far behind us," Slocum said. "What do you think happened to him?"

"I think he's dead," Crawford told them. Crawford lifted his canteen from his saddle. He shook it, to see how much water was left. Not much. He unscrewed the cap and took a drink. "The fool. I warned him to be careful, when he started falling behind with that damn horse of his."

Slocum said, "That's Kingsley for you. He never did know how to take care of no horse."

Neither Slocum nor Werdann missed Kingsley. Kingsley had been a small-time criminal and saloon fighter, a bully who thought with his fists.

Werdann shifted uneasily. His tight, thin-soled cowboy boots hurt his feet when there was a lot of walking to be done, as there had been today. "You figure Apaches got him?"

"Or Honeycutt," Crawford said.

"Honeycutt!" said Werdann.

Crawford took another drink, then he replaced the canteen on his saddle horn. "I've been expecting Honeycutt to come after us. I just didn't think he could catch us this soon."

"But why Honeycutt?" Werdann persisted. "He's the one that put us on to Slater, and all."

"Why do you think?" Crawford asked sarcastically. "Money. A fellow like Honeycutt may say that all he wants to do is kill Slater and become The Regulator; but sooner or later, those dollar signs are going to start flashing in front of his eyes. He's a bounty hunter, and we're bounty."

"That's right," said Slocum. "And it won't hurt his regulatin' reputation none if he kills him the leader of the scalp hunters."

Crawford nodded. "Precisely. So either we finish him off now, or we spend the rest of our lives looking over our shoulders for him. To tell the truth, I've been planning for this. I intended to wait for Honeycutt at that cantina at the end of the *Jornada*, and kill him there." He grinned at his companions. "You see, even if he wasn't after us, he'll be carrying Slater's head. We'll relieve him of it and turn it in for the reward. That's two thousand dollars, in addition to what we'll get for these scalps. Enough to keep us going for a while."

"You sure he'll have Slater's head?" Werdann said.

"He'll have it. He showed me the jar he meant to put it in."

"I mean, are you sure he was able to find Slater and kill him?"

Slocum answered before Crawford could. "Jesus, Werdann. You saw Slater. He was more dead than alive when we left him on them anthills. He couldn't have gone very far. He couldn't have took on a five-year-old, much less somebody like that big bastard Honeycutt."

Werdann said, "It's still hard to believe it's Honeycutt after us, not with that horse we give him."

Slocum bit off a fingernail with his bad teeth. He spit out the nail and the dirt that had come with it. "Maybe he got another horse, somehow. He was capable of anything."

Werdann sneered at him. "You sound like you're scared of him."

"Shut up, Werdann. You think 'cause you was a hired gun for them Texas ranchers, you're some kind of hot shit. You think you're better'n everybody else in the outfit."

"Maybe I do," Werdann admitted. He had ridden for some of the big Texas cattle spreads, in their feuds with incoming farmers and with each other. When the law had come in, and work had gotten scarce, he'd drifted west. He said, "What I did, it was like a profession. It was honorable, kind of. We had us a code."

Slocum scoffed. "Shootin' grangers in the back? Some code."

"At least I only done men, and most of them was looking to do me first. I didn't kill no women. I didn't kill my wife. I didn't kill that whore in Denver and chop her into pieces."

Slocum's heavy lower lip trembled. Back in Ohio, Slocum had been a freight driver. One night, in a fit of drunken jealousy, he had killed his unfaithful wife. Even worse, he had found that he enjoyed doing it. He had fled west, where he had become a bar bouncer and loan collector. Then he'd gotten drunk again and killed the Denver prostitute. He'd enjoyed that, too, especially cutting her up. Western society didn't pay much attention to the murder of prostitutes, but it objected to mutilation, so Slocum had fled to Santa Fe, one step ahead of Judge Lynch. There, he'd met Crawford and joined the scalp hunters.

To Werdann, Slocum retorted, "I notice your fancy code don't stop you from killing Apache women, or their kids."

"All right," Werdann amended, "I don't kill *white* women. It ain't like Injuns is real people, after all. Hell, even niggers is more like people than Injuns." He sniffed. "Anyway, when I kill Injuns, or anybody else, it's business. I do it for money. You do it 'cause you like it. You ain't right in the head, Slocum."

Before Slocum could reply, Crawford said, "Stop squabbling, you two, and let me think. You're like a couple of schoolboys."

He took his horse's reins from Werdann. "Come on, let's get moving."

The three men mounted their horses. The leather bag full of Apache scalps still hung from Crawford's saddle horn.

As they started off, Crawford theorized aloud. "Somebody's following us, we know that. It's either Apaches or Honeycutt." He looked back once. "I wish I had Sam Slater's nose. He could smell the bastards and tell you who they were."

"That's a damn Injun trick," Slocum said.

Werdann said, "Slater was part Injun, what I heard."

"Well, now he's all dead," Slocum said. "Serves him right, too, what he done to us—what he done to Quirt Evans. Quirt and me was pals."

"That don't surprise me," Werdann said, in a voice tinged with disgust.

Slocum bristled. "What the hell you mean by that?"

"Enough, I said," Crawford told them. "Why don't we just kill each other, and make it easier for whoever's back there?"

In his mind's eye, Crawford pictured the country between here and Dead Man's Tanks, and after that, to Martin Cruz's cantina. "Whoever it is, we're going to prepare a little surprise for him."

Slocum said, "You said before we was going to take him out at that cantina."

"I changed my mind. I didn't expect him to catch up to us this fast. I thought we'd have time to get to the cantina and wait for him. After Dead Man's Tanks, the land flattens out. I'd rather ambush him in the hills than have him catch us out on the flats. I want to make sure the initiative stays with us."

Werdann said, "What if it ain't Honeycutt after us? What if it's Apaches?"

"My sixth sense tells me it's Honeycutt," Crawford said. "But even if it isn't, that doesn't change the plan."

"Which is?"

"We're going to fort up at the Tanks. We can wait there a long time. Whoever's after us can't. Eventually they'll have to come for water. Then they'll be ours. You've been to the Tanks, you remember the trail? It winds up that steep canyon. About three-quarters of the way down the canyon, there's a bench where you can look out over the approaches and see, hell, it must be forty miles. Nobody can get near the place without our knowing about it. And when they come . . . " He drew his thumb across his throat.

"Can't they get at us from behind?" Slocum said.

Crawford shook his head, smiling like the cat that found the cream. "There's a sheer cliff. They come at us from the front, or not at all. I want to get to the Tanks before dark. We'll take care of the horses and get water for ourselves, then we'll set up our little reception. Honeycutt's done a hell of a job to catch up to us like this, but I'm afraid that all it's going to get him is an early grave. Mr. Honeycutt isn't quite as clever as he thinks he is."

Crawford's smile turned into a grin, then he laughed out loud. The three scalp hunters rode on.

CHAPTER 21

THE MOUNTAIN IN WHOSE CANYON RECESSES lay the *tinaja* known as Dead Man's Tanks rose from the desert like an *Arabian Nights* fortress. Fantastically carved pinnacles and crenellations of rock reached high into the sky. The canyon wound into this stronghold through a wide opening in the mountain's southwestern side. Supposedly, it was the only way a man might enter. On this particular day, however, an astute observer might have spied a lone figure climbing the mountain's eastern wall.

Sam Slater had remembered the canyon entrance to the Tanks. He was afraid that the scalp hunters might be on the lookout for

Kingsley, or for whoever had caused Kingsley to disappear. Sam had decided to come to the Tanks by a way the scalp hunters wouldn't expect. He had decided to come the Apache way.

He had started his climb in the late afternoon. By nightfall, he was only halfway to the top. Sam's shirt was still tied around his waist. His rifle was slung across his back, along with the water skin. He had need of both his hands. He could not go as fast as he might have liked, because he was still feverish from his ordeal on the anthill and tired from the long chase across the *Jornada*. He followed fissures and crevices in the dark, feeling his way. The faint moonlight was some help, but not much. He wanted to be over the top and near the Tanks before dawn. Then he would move on the scalp hunters.

In places, the rock was nearly vertical. Sam had to scale it, feeling for handholds and footholds, at times hanging on by his fingertips and toes. He was only too aware that a misplaced hand or foot could send him plummeting to the talus below. He pictured himself bouncing off the rocks like a rag doll, the way Paulsen had, when he and his horse had fallen from the rock ledge during the retreat from the Apache village. He remembered Paulsen's screams. He tried to get the picture out of his mind, to concentrate on what he was doing. He was an Apache. An Apache could climb anything.

He left the rock wall and picked his way along a

boulder-strewn incline. There was a cool breeze up here, far above the desert floor. Above him, a tall pinnacle of rock was silhouetted against the stars. Flat rocks were laid across the pinnacle's top, like a giant table. Sam wondered what processes of wind and water had sculpted such a formation.

As Sam neared the pinnacle, he had to scramble up an immense slab of rock. Then the breeze swirled all around his sweaty body, and he knew he had reached the top.

He tried to get his bearings, to figure out where he was in relation to the Tanks. It was hard to tell in the dark. He'd planned it so that he could go over the top and then straight down, but he'd been forced to angle sideways during the climb, and he wasn't sure where he had ended up. The table-top pinnacle hadn't been visible from the spot on the desert floor where he'd begun his ascent.

He swore. He hadn't planned on taking so long to get to the top, and now he wasn't sure where he was. If, after all this, he missed Crawford and the other two; if by the time he got to the Tanks, they'd broken camp and ridden out . . .

He swore again. He'd never catch them, in that case. He was stiff and sore from the climb. He was exhausted from running all day. He'd never be able to put forth that kind of effort again. He should have waited for darkness and gone up the canyon, he thought. He should have taken his chances.

He drank from his water skin, then began

working his way down the mountain. The going was almost as steep on this side of the mountain, though there were no more vertical drops.

As he moved through the rock, the land began to take a definite slope to his right. The canyon must be that way. The Tanks were near the canyon's head.

He followed the slope of the land, taking pains to be quiet. He soon found himself in the canyon. He was downwind. Good. The scalp hunters' horses would not pick up his scent.

The short summer night was coming to an end. Sam couldn't see the eastern horizon from here, but he knew that dawn must be breaking, or close to it. He hoped that for once Crawford and his men hadn't left camp early. He hurried now, unslinging Honeycutt's Smith & Wesson hunting rifle and carrying it in his hand. Was it his imagination or was there a faint lightening of the darkness around him? Yes, it was dawn.

As he neared the canyon bottom, he recognized the landscape from his first trip out here. The Tanks were just ahead. There was the spreading ironwood tree. Sam stopped. The scalp hunters wouldn't be camped right at the Tanks, but a little ways off. Sam bet that they'd pick the same place he and Crawford had used.

Sam cut a wide circle, heading for the campground. Every now and then he stopped to listen. He heard nothing, nothing but the song of an early rising cactus wren. He pressed an ear to the ground. There was no faint rumble of hoofbeats to tell him that the scalp hunters were riding out of the canyon. Either they had left much earlier, or they were still here.

As Sam neared the campground, he smelled horses. A thin smile crossed his lips.

He crept slowly among the rocks. Around him, the dawn had turned everything a flat shade of gray. The air was cool, in contrast to the terrible heat that would soon follow. Sam smelled the fragrant dew, what little of it there was. He smelled the stagnant water in the Tanks.

Then he smelled something else—the remains of a fire. It was the first fire the scalp hunters had built since leaving the old mission. That was odd.

Sam heard the horses now, stamping their hoofs, blowing. They were picketed in the same draw that he and Crawford had used before.

Sam let the fire's odor guide him to the scalp hunters' campground. Edging around a boulder, he saw the gray remains of the fire. He saw the scalp hunters' saddles and their neatly rolled bedding.

He didn't see the scalp hunters.

A chill ran up Sam's back. He didn't like this.

He looked around, half expecting to find them behind him, to find himself trapped. But he was alone.

He watched the camp for a while. He was in no hurry, now. The scalp hunters weren't going anywhere without their horses.

No one appeared.

At last, Sam advanced out of the rocks, his finger on the hunting rifle's trigger. He knelt by the fire and examined the ashes. From the looks of things, they had built the fire last night—built it good and big, too—then let it burn down. It was as if they had wanted to advertise their presence. Why?

Sam moved around the camp. It was easy to pick out the scalp hunters' footprints, three different sets of them. Circling out from the fire, Sam found that the most recent prints led back down the canyon, in a group. He began to have an idea what they might be up to.

Sam went back to the Tanks. He brushed aside the scummy water and took a long drink. He refilled his water skin, then he moved down the canyon, following the scalp hunters' footprints. He was alert, quiet. The canyon was just as silent.

He reached the point where the canyon turned and opened up. The view was panoramic. In the distance, the first rays of the morning sun spread across the desert floor, bathing the high points in soft golden light, while the rest remained in shadow. Already it was getting warmer.

Sam stopped, squatting. He ran his eyes across the broken ground, quartering it.

Then he saw one of them. It was Slocum. He was crouched in some rocks, scratching himself. Not far away, Sam saw Crawford, waiting with his rifle. Across the canyon and just above those two was the Texan, Werdann.

They were waiting for Sam, or whoever they thought had caught up to Kingsley. They must know that Kingsley wasn't coming, by now. They must know that they were being followed, and they had decided to ambush their pursuer, or pursuers. All three were looking down the canyon, watching the entrance.

As Sam watched, Slocum shifted in the rocks. His voice sounded concerned. "Ain't nobody out there, Colonel."

"There will be," Crawford said confidently. "He'll come. He has to. God himself would eventually have to come to water out here, and this is the only water for thirty miles."

Sam thought about shooting them. No, he'd only be able to get one, then the other two would be alerted. Besides, they were wedged into the rocks so well that hitting them at this distance would be chancy. Better to move in close and try to take them one by one.

Werdann was the highest up, the closest to him. The Texan sat between two great slabs of rock, watching patiently—but then this probably wasn't the first time he'd participated in an ambush. He would know how to wait. Sam decided to take him first.

Sam worked down and to his right, along the canyon wall. He moved slowly, stealthily, taking care where he put his moccasined feet, lest he knock loose some stones and give away his presence. The sun's rays were creeping over the canyon's far wall, now. The desert below was awash in bright light.

Sam looked away from Werdann as he closed in on him. A man could feel it when someone was staring at his back. The canyon was getting like an oven, as hot air rose from the desert floor. Sam ached all over. His upper body was in agony from being staked on the anthills. The dirt he'd rubbed all over himself yesterday hadn't made his wounds feel any better, either.

He was ten yards from Werdann now, above and behind him. There was a gravelly open space between the two men. Sam stopped. He couldn't get any closer without making noise.

Sam drew the Mexican *cuchillo* from his belt. He balanced it by its long blade. He aimed, drew back his arm, and threw.

The knife sped through the air, turning over once. The blade embedded itself in Werdann's neck, at the base of his skull.

The Texan straightened, grabbing for the knife, trying to pull it out. He stood, almost involuntarily, as if his body were acting independently of his brain. Still trying to pull out the knife, he staggered from between the rocks. Then he toppled onto his face.

There was a shout, followed by a rifle shot. A bullet whined off the rock near Sam's face and he threw himself down.

So much for taking them one by one.

CHAPTER 22

SAM SCRAMBLED INTO THE ROCKS, FOR BETter cover.

Below him, Slocum glimpsed a headband and a bare brown chest. “It ain’t Honeycutt,” he yelled. “It’s an Apache!”

Behind some nearby rocks, Crawford levered another shell into the chamber of his Winchester. “No, it’s not,” he cried back. “It’s Slater!”

“Slater?” said Slocum. “That’s impossible. Slater’s dead.”

“Then he has a very active ghost. If you don’t believe me, go up and take a closer look. Be careful, though, because he’s liable to do to you what he just did to Werdann.”

Slocum searched the rugged hillside for a sign of their quarry. "How the hell could it be Slater? And how did he get in here without us seeing him?"

Crawford said, "Worry about that later, will you? Right now, let's kill him."

Above them, Sam wriggled through the rocks. On the far side of the gravelly open space, he saw Werdann. The Texan was still twitching weakly, the long *cuchillo* sticking out of his neck.

There was no sound from the other two scalp hunters. Sam knew they must be communicating with hand signals, now. He guessed what they would do. One of them would attempt to pin him down, while the other maneuvered and tried to get a good shot at him. They would try to get him in a cross fire. He poked the hunting rifle through the rocks. He couldn't see either of them.

There was a shot. Sam ducked instinctively. Crawford's voice sounded, from a different spot than he'd heard it a minute earlier. "Sam! Is that you?"

"It's me," Sam called back.

"How did you get here?"

"I took the train. What do you think?"

There was another shot. This time Sam fought instinct and didn't duck. He tried to see where the bullet had come from.

"What happened to Honeycutt?" Crawford yelled.

"He had a problem with his head," Sam replied.

"His head?"

"He heard bells ringing."

There was a shot from another direction. Sam saw the powder smoke, but he had no target for return fire.

"Did you kill Kingsley?" Crawford cried.

Sam didn't answer. He couldn't stay here talking. He'd be playing into their hands. He looked around. Above him was a flat-topped rock projection. From there, he could cover the lower part of the canyon. He could look down on Slocum and Crawford.

Sam broke cover. He ran for the base of the projection, dodging among the rocks. Behind him, the two scalp hunters opened fire. Bullets hummed around Sam's ears. They whined off the rocks nearby. Suddenly, Sam's back and hips were drenched with water. One of the razor-sharp rock chips had shredded the steer's intestine that was slung over his back. From below he heard a triumphal cry. The scalp hunters had seen.

Sam swore savagely. He was without water. He tried to go back and get Werdann's canteen.

Too late. Crawford and Slocum had already reached Werdann's position. They fired at Sam, and he was forced to retreat. He should have taken Werdann's canteen after he had killed him. You could never have too much water in this country. That had been a mistake, and Sam was afraid he was going to pay for it.

He reached the bottom of the rock projection. A deep fissure in the granite led to the top. Sam slipped inside the fissure and began to climb. For the moment, he was hidden from the scalp hunters. The danger would come when he emerged on top. The water that dripped down his back cooled him in the heat. It was about the only good he would get from it.

He reached the top and climbed out, rolling as bullets spattered the rock around him. He took up a firing position. Both Crawford and Slocum were in view below him, advancing. He fired at Crawford. He heard an oath and saw the scalp hunter grab his ear. Then Crawford and Slocum went to earth.

Sam shrugged off the punctured water skin and threw it away. The shirt that he had rolled around his waist was soaked. He took it off and began squeezing it into his mouth, sucking the water from the fabric, trying to get as much of the precious liquid into him before the shirt dried in the furnacelike heat. The water tasted salty from all the sweat that had soaked into the shirt. It was gritty with dirt.

There was a rifle shot. The bullet screamed off the face of the rock ledge. Sam heard distant footsteps, and looked out just in time to see Slocum running and diving for cover. It was too late to get a good shot at him, so Sam held his fire.

He continued sucking water out of the shirt. He was going to be out here a long time in this heat, and this dirty water might mean the difference between life and death. He looked out. The scalp hunters were retreating back down the canyon, moving from cover to cover. Sam squeezed off a shot at Slocum. He missed, but the jowly scalp hunter dove awkwardly behind some rocks, and Sam heard a yelp.

"You hit?" Crawford called.

"No, goddammit," growled Slocum. "I landed in some cactus. One plant in this hellhole, and I got to fall on it."

Sam had gotten himself in a commanding defensive position, but it was now irrelevant. The scalp hunters were doing the smart thing. They were doing what Sam himself would have done. They were moving to block Sam from the Tanks. There was no other water within a day's ride. Eventually, Sam would be forced to go for water. He would have to go to the Tanks. He would have to go to Crawford and Slocum.

"Hey, Sam!" It was Crawford.

Sam didn't answer.

"Sam, it's awful hot out here, isn't it?"

Sam said nothing. Crawford wanted him to reply. Shouting in this heat would make him thirstier.

Crawford went on. "Sam, if you're thirsty, we've got enough water to go around. I'm having some right now, in fact, and it certainly is good." The scalp hunter's laughter rang off the canyon walls.

The sun beat down into the canyon with full force now. The rocks on which Sam lay were heating up. They wouldn't get hot enough to fry eggs—that was a myth—but they would get too hot for him to lie on.

He should find a patch of shade. He should hole up until dark, conserving himself, then make his move. That was what an Apache would do. Only an insane man—or a stupid one—would rush the scalp hunters in the daylight.

But Sam had only been adopted by the Apaches; he wasn't full-blooded. Those men out there had gotten his dander up. He wanted to kill them, and he didn't feel like waiting around all day to do it.

He put on the wet shirt. It would help to cool him for a bit. Then he picked up his rifle, and he went on the attack.

CHAPTER 23

THE TWO SCALP HUNTERS HAD TAKEN UP positions on either side of the canyon. Slocum was on the left, Crawford on the right. The canyon slopes were a mass of boulders and crevices, providing good cover. Slocum was the weak link. Sam decided to work on him first.

Sam advanced from rock to rock, always making sure of his next move before he took it. He climbed the canyon wall, trying to get above Slocum. The two scalp hunters fired at him. Then they moved as well, back up the canyon, not wanting Sam to get behind them.

Sam went higher up the canyon wall. Slocum and Crawford fired and moved back again.

Despite all that he'd been through, Sam was in better shape than Slocum. He could move faster. He counted on these qualities to give him an advantage down the line.

Slowly, the battle moved back toward the Tanks. Sam advanced on Slocum. First Slocum fired at him, then Crawford, while Slocum retreated to a better position. After a few minutes, Sam moved again, with the same results. It was an elegantly choreographed dance of death. The scalp hunters knew that Sam didn't have any water. Their strategy was to tire him out, to wear him down in the blistering heat.

It was good strategy.

The water on Sam's shirt dried. His whole body dried. He sucked pebbles as he fought. Both scalp hunters had full canteens, and they were retreating toward a source of water. Sam would have to kill them to get a drink.

When Sam got a good shot at Slocum or Crawford, he took it. He didn't take many, though. The Apaches had taught him to conserve ammunition. Both scalp hunters blazed away at Sam whenever he showed himself. Crawford was the best shot, but he was farthest away. During one of Slocum's retreats, Sam wounded him, hitting him in the upper leg. The next time Sam saw the scalp hunter, he had tied his bandana around the wound, as a bandage.

Afternoon stillness descended on the canyon, disturbed only by an occasional flurry of gunshots that echoed off the rock walls. The three men drew nearer to the Tanks. The lure of the water was so great that Sam had to force himself to think what he was doing. He had to force himself not to go straight in and drink. In the heat, without a hat, with no water, he was beginning to suffer dizzy spells. He had to stop until the spells passed, and he could go on once more.

When he had drawn nearly level with Slocum, he stopped running and began to crawl, wriggling unseen among the rocks and boulders. Slocum's last position had been on a platformlike rock overhang. Sam crawled past the overhang, inching along, then he worked his way down the canyon side. He hoped to take Slocum from the rear, to catch him looking the other way.

Crawling over the sharp, gravelly soil was agony on Sam's injured chest, but he endured it. He moved slowly,watchfully, the hunting rifle cradled in the crook of his arms. The scalp hunters must be wondering where he had gone, what he was up to. Maybe they thought they'd hit him.

The rocks blocked almost all view as Sam neared the overhang. He licked his lips. His tongue was dry and raspy, like a cat's. He listened intently, heard nothing. He crawled closer. Slocum was still there; Sam smelled the man's rank odor.

Sam stood. With the Smith & Wesson leveled, he stepped around a rock and onto the overhang.

Slocum heard him and turned.

Sam fired a fraction of a second before Slocum did. Slocum's bullet tore through Sam's shirt, grazing his ribs. Sam's bullet caught Slocum in the chest. "Ow!" yelled Slocum, doubling over. His rifle fell from his hands, off the overhang, and down the steep slope to the canyon floor.

Slocum stumbled to his knees, holding his wound, trying to staunch the bleeding. There was blood on his bandaged leg, as well. He looked up at Sam. "Come on, Slater. Help me. There's still time."

Their eyes met. Slocum's eyes were pleading, Sam's were cold. With his foot, Sam pushed Slocum off the overhang. The scalp hunter's screams rang through the canyon as he fell.

Slocum's canteen lay on the overhang. Sam picked it up. Fumbling with anticipation, he unscrewed the cap. Still holding his rifle, he raised the canteen to his lips.

There was a shot. The rifle was knocked from Sam's hand by the impact of the bullet, and the wooden canteen shattered. Sam ducked for cover. From the direction of the shot, he knew that Crawford had crossed the canyon, then gotten above and behind him. He hadn't expected him to do that. Crawford hadn't been wondering where Sam was; he'd had it figured out all along. He'd left Slocum out there as a decoy.

By a strange coincidence, Crawford's bullet

had hit the rifle and had been deflected into the canteen, which had literally exploded from the bullet's impact. The rifle's receiver was smashed. Keeping the rifle in his hand had saved Sam's life. Otherwise, the bullet would have hit him.

Sam's hands and forearms dripped with water. He sucked them dry, getting what little of the precious moisture he could, swearing at Crawford's luck.

From the rocks above, less than a hundred yards off, came Crawford's boyish laughter. "Sorry about the water, Sam."

"Apologies noted," Sam cried back. He drew his pistol. He couldn't stay on the overhang. There was nowhere to maneuver. He'd be trapped, just as Slocum had been.

"It's just you and me now, Sam," Crawford cried. "I don't want to shoot you."

Sam timed his move off the overhang. He dived behind a neighboring rock as Crawford's bullet kicked up dirt just behind him.

"I thought we were friends," Crawford went on.

"There was a time I thought so, too," Sam replied. "I reckon you were as close to a friend as I've had."

"Well, then, what's the matter? I saved your life twice, remember?"

"You also tried to kill me," Sam said.

"You came here to kill me, too, remember that," said Crawford. "So why don't we call it even and start over?"

"You killed Teresa, Crawford. That more than makes up for anything good you ever did."

"Teresa? She was just a little Mexican bitch. Hell, she wasn't even all Mex. She was part Indian. You're not going to let her come between us, are you?"

"She was a human being, Crawford. She was a woman. She trusted you. She didn't deserve to die like that."

"What else could I do with her? When we went back to the anthills and you were gone, I knew right away she had set you loose. I knew she had fired those shots to make us think the Apaches were attacking. She admitted it, too, after we had questioned her for a while. Hell, Sam, do you think I didn't know that you and she were lovers? I know everything that goes on with my men. But I didn't care, Sam—don't you see? Because you were my *friend.*"

Crawford continued. "Teresa had to die. She had gone against the group. She had gone against me. If I hadn't killed her, no one would have listened to me anymore. But there is no more group, now. We can start over. You and me."

Sam had to keep going, he had to get some room to maneuver. He circled out from the rocks, moving uphill. Crawford was moving, too. They saw each other. Crawford fired his rifle at Sam. Sam wasted a pistol shot, just to keep the scalp hunter's head down.

From out of sight, Crawford said, "Come on,

Sam. I've got a bag full of Apache scalps back there. You and I can split the money for them, fifty-fifty. Hell, we can take Slocum and Werdann in and collect the bounty on them, too. That's another thousand. We can even say that Werdann was me and make it five thousand. That's a lot of money, Sam. What do you say?"

Sam kept circling up the hill. "No deal, Crawford."

There was a brief pause, then Crawford said, "I'm sorry to hear that, Sam. I'm going to hate killing you."

Sam's reply was a bullet that made Crawford jump and move downhill to new cover.

The two men stalked each other. Neither was sure where the other was. Sam had his pistol cocked and ready. He was at a disadvantage, because Crawford had the longer-range rifle. The sun beat down. The only sounds were Sam's hoarse breathing and the faint scraping of his moccasins against the gravel of the slope.

Sam could see the Tanks now, on their apron of worn rock. The sight of the Tanks heightened his thirst, but he could not go to the water without exposing himself and being shot. Neither could Crawford, but Crawford had at least some water left in his canteen.

Sam worked to his left and down, hoping to cut Crawford off. But he didn't see him. He came back to the right, every sense alert, his hand sweating on the pistol's wooden grip.

He heard a faint noise, below him and to the right.

He stopped. He didn't hear the noise again. There was no way of telling which way the scalp hunter was moving. For that reason, Sam couldn't circle the noise, the way an Apache would. He had to go straight toward it.

He inched along, hugging the hot face of a granite dome. He rounded a corner, pistol pointed. Crawford rounded the dome at the same moment, not twenty yards off. Both men fired their weapons and ducked back behind cover. The gunshots and the whine of bullets off rock echoed through the canyon.

Sam studied the massive granite formation that separated him from Crawford. He slipped his pistol into his belt and hoisted himself up the rock. He reached the top and squatted there, catching his breath and listening for Crawford.

He heard nothing. He drew the pistol and moved across the dome's uneven surface in a crouch. He moved silently, looking over the rock's top for Crawford. He didn't see or hear him. Where was the bastard?

Then he saw him, moving away from the dome, heading downhill toward the Tanks.

Sam started toward him, leveling his pistol. He must have made a noise, or else Crawford had a sixth sense, because at that moment Crawford looked up and saw him.

Sam pointed the pistol and pulled the trigger.

Click. Misfire.

No time for another shot. Sam threw the pistol at Crawford and leaped off the rock at him. The hurled pistol threw off Crawford's reflex shot. Sam felt the rifle's hot blast on his cheek as he landed on the scalp hunter.

The two men rolled down the steep slope of the canyon, head over heel, tearing clothes and skin, bouncing off sharp rocks. Sam landed about a quarter of the way from the bottom, near the Tanks. He shook his head, momentarily dazed. He tried to stand. Crawford was a little above him. Crawford got to his feet first. Both of Crawford's pistols had fallen from their holsters in the tumble down the hill. Crawford picked up a rock and ran at Sam, swinging the rock at Sam's head.

Sam ducked, throwing himself at Crawford's feet. Crawford missed with the rock and went over Sam's back. Sam threw himself on the scalp hunter. They rolled the rest of the way down the hill. Crawford got free. Sam got up, and Crawford threw a shoulder into him, knocking him back down. Crawford drew the knife from his belt. Sam's own knife was gone. Before Crawford could set himself, Sam kicked the knife from his hand. Instinctively, Crawford looked to see where the weapon had gone. Sam charged in on him, catching him in the stomach, knocking him down. Crawford used Sam's own momentum to throw Sam over onto his back.

Both men scrambled up. Crawford hit Sam

flush in the nose, breaking it. Sam felt blood run down his face. Crawford swung at Sam again. This time Sam blocked the punch and followed with a right hand that rocked Crawford.

Sam moved forward. Crawford saw something, turned, and ran for it. Sam saw it too—sunlight glinting off metal. One of the pistols.

Sam ran after Crawford. Just as Crawford reached the pistol, Sam tackled him from behind. Both men went sliding forward in the dirt. Crawford's outstretched hand reached for the pistol. Sam caught the hand. He knocked the pistol loose and flicked it out of the scalp hunter's reach. Crawford rolled over and threw dirt at Sam's eyes. Sam ducked the dirt. He hit Crawford in the face. He hit him again. Crawford tried to fight back, but Sam overwhelmed him, with blow after blow, until the scalp hunter was unconscious, blood all over his face.

Sam crawled off of Crawford, who moaned, stirring faintly. Sam was exhausted, dizzy, delirious from heat and thirst. He had to breathe through his mouth. Blood poured from his nose, but he was used to that. The nose had been busted so many times, it broke in a high wind, anymore.

He looked around. The pistol had skidded onto the smooth rock at the edge of the Tanks. He crawled toward it, oblivious to anything else. He picked up the pistol, cocking it, wanting only to shoot Crawford and get it over with. As he turned toward the scalp hunter, a pair of moccasined feet stepped in front of him.

Sam looked up. The feet belonged to an Apache Indian, and at first Sam thought that the Indian was part of his delirium. There was still a lot of black in the Indian's hair, though Sam knew that the man was at least seventy. The Indian's lined and wrinkled face looked down at Sam without pity. He wore a U.S. Army officer's jacket, unbuttoned, and a long breech-clout. In one hand was a Winchester repeating rifle; at his waist was a Colt .45. He was accompanied by at least a dozen men, armed and painted for war.

Sam realized that the Indian was no dream, and he let out his breath. "Greetings, *Nantan*," he said. "Greetings, Chief."

CHAPTER 24

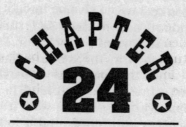

NANAY LOOKED FROM SAM TO CRAWFORD. The old chief wast all for an Indian, and frail looking. In the tribe he was called Broken Foot, because of a crippled ankle, but never to his face. Many said he was the greatest of all Apache war chiefs. He was responsible for far more white deaths than the more celebrated leaders, like Cochise and Victorio.

The other Indians stood or squatted in the rocks, or in the cool shade of the ironwood tree. They were armed with rifles and pistols, and they looked ready, even eager, to use their weapons.

Sam didn't drop his pistol, nor did the Apaches

tell him to. They didn't have to. They knew as well as he did that he had no chance to fight his way out of this. One shot was all he would get, if he was lucky, and then he would be dead.

Nanay turned his dark eyes back on Sam and nodded imperceptibly. "I did not expect to find the son of my old friend here." Sam's Apache name was Scar, but Apaches considered it rude to use personal names in addressing one another, except under certain unusual circumstances. Nanay had known Sam's adoptive father, Loco. The two men had been friends, but that friendship wouldn't keep Sam alive a second longer, if Nanay decided that he should die.

Sam stood slowly. He had a hard time breathing, because of his broken nose. He spit blood from his mouth; he wiped more blood on the back of his hand. He said, "How long were you watching, *Nantan?*"

"A long time," said the old man. "I like to watch the *nancin* fight among themselves."

The other Apaches laughed. *Nancin* was the warpath name for Americans or Mexicans.

"How did you get here?" asked Sam.

"We climbed the mountain. We followed your tracks."

Sam figured that they must have left their horses on the other side of the mountain.

Sam looked at the unconscious Crawford. "You know who that man is?"

"I know who he is. I know what he has done

to my people. It is you that I wonder about. I wonder what the *yodascin* has become."

Sam knew that he was on trial, in a court every bit as powerful, and far more deadly, than any he had faced in the white man's world. He said, "I was with those men, *Nantan,* it is true, but I was not one of them. I took no scalps. I pretended to be one of them, in order to gain their confidence. It was I who warned your camp of the scalp hunters' attack. I came to this country to destroy their band. The white men will pay me much money for doing this."

Nanay looked doubtful. "The white man will pay to stop the killing of the *Dine?* That does not sound like the white men I have known."

"The whites have their reasons, *Nantan.* This man and his band have killed more than *Dine.* They break the white men's laws, as well as those of the Apache. The whites want them brought to justice."

The old Apache took a turn around the rocks, limping with his arthritic stride. It must hurt him just to move, but he did not show it. Sam couldn't imagine how he had scaled the mountain. Nanay was absolutely fearless. He knew that if Sam fought, he would be the first to die, yet he came back and stood inches from Sam. He said, "We followed two sets of tracks from the village of the Spanish priests. From the tracks, my people thought that the *nancin* were being followed by one of our own. I was not so sure. The moccasin prints were those of an Apache, but something in the stride reminded me of a white man. Now I see the *yodascin*, and I know why."

Sam said nothing.

Nanay went on, "The big yellow-hair at the Spanish village. You killed him?"

"Yes, *Nantan*."

"We found the remains of a woman, also. She was your woman?"

Sam hesitated. He might as well tell the truth. It would do no good to lie to a man like Nanay. But what was the truth?

"Yes, *Nantan*, she was mine. At least, she wanted to be mine, but I would not let her. She would have come with me, if I had tried harder to make her. And because I did not try, she went back to this man"—he nodded toward Crawford—"and he did . . . you saw what he did to her. Her fate was my responsibility."

"These men tortured you as well, did they not?" Nanay said.

"Yes, *Nantan*."

"Because of the woman?"

"Because they found out why I had come to them. It was the woman who saved me."

The old Indian looked closely at Sam, studying him. At last, he spoke. "All that you say may be true, my friend, or it may be that you were one of these people and had a falling out over the woman."

"That's right, Nanay," said a new voice. It

was Crawford, sitting up now. "It was all because of the girl. Slater was one of us. He took as many scalps as any of us."

One of Crawford's eyes was swollen shut. His face was bruised and puffy, and there was blood in his mouth. There was dried blood on his left shoulder, where his ear had bled after being grazed by Sam's bullet. He looked at Sam with a smug grin.

Nanay stared at Crawford coldly, then turned away. The Apaches conferred among themselves. They seemed to be arguing, and Sam knew that boded ill for him. It would do him no good to beg for his life. It would even be counterproductive, for the Apaches would take it as a sign of guilt.

When the Indians had finished talking, Nanay turned back to Sam. Sam fingered the pistol in his sweaty hand. Nanay had such presence that Sam didn't think he'd have the nerve to shoot him. Sam said, "What will you do with us, *Nantan?*"

Nanay nodded toward Crawford. "*That* man, we will take back to our camp. We will give him to our women. They may deal with him as they choose."

Sam's bowels went cold. Apache women were notoriously more ferocious than the men. The grin faded from Crawford's face. He got to his feet. "No. No," he begged. He looked to Sam for help.

Sam's words sounded as though they were coming from a great distance. "And me?"

Once more, Nanay's wizened visage turned on Sam. The dark eyes looked into his. "These warriors say that you lie. They want you to suffer the same fate as the *nancin*. But I have always known my friend's son, the *yodascin*, to tell the truth. Whether they are correct or I, it is impossible to say. Therefore, we will let Ussen, Creator of Life, decide your fate."

He went on, "You shall be left here, without horse, or food, or weapons, or vessels to carry water. If you survive the desert, then *enjuh*, it is good. If not, you have lied to us."

Sam let out his breath. At least he had a chance. At least they weren't going to take him back to their camp. Better to die the torture of thirst on the *Jornada*, than to die at the hands of the Apache women.

"Now, my friend, you must give me the pistol," ordered Nanay.

Panic stricken, Crawford said, "Christ, Sam. Don't let them do this to me. Shoot me. Kill me, please. Please God, Sam, I'm white, like you. Don't let them take me back to their women. You know what they'll do to me."

Sam didn't know, not for sure, but he could guess. It wouldn't be pretty, and it would take a long time. The anthills might seem like a picnic in comparison.

Nanay seemed to read Sam's mind. Reluctantly, he said, "The *nancin* begs you to kill him. You know that, by our laws, you may claim that right. You were the victor in your fight with that man. It was a fair fight, and you have the right to dispose of him as you will. Either way, justice will be done."

Crawford looked relieved. "Come on, Sam. Get it over with, before they change their minds."

Sam looked from Crawford to Nanay, and back again.

"Hurry up, Sam," Crawford said.

Sam let down the pistol's hammer. He twirled the weapon once.

Crawford cried, "Sam . . . !"

Sam said, "Sorry, Crawford."

"Sam, think what they'll do to me."

"I am thinking. I'm thinking what you did to Teresa, and to all those women and children back at the village, and to those Mexican sheepherders."

Crawford moved forward. "Sam!"

With animal swiftness, the Apache warriors cut him off. They grabbed Crawford's arms and dragged him away, to the draw where the horses waited. Crawford struggled in the Indians' grasp. He looked back at Sam, and his once-boyish features were contorted with fear and rage.

"I'll see you in hell, Slater!"

"Maybe," said Sam, "but you'll get there first."

Sam faced Nanay. He handed him the pistol.

The old Indian looked at Sam. For the first time his dark eyes softened. "May we live long enough to meet each other again," he said.

Sam nodded in reply.

Nanay turned and left. In the background, Crawford's terrified cries echoed above the Tanks.

The Apaches left the canyon with the blubbering Crawford, taking the scalp hunters' horses with them, stopping to retrieve the white men's canteens and weapons.

Then they were gone, and Sam was alone. The sun beat down. Sam had started this journey with few assets, now he had even less. All he had were two bodies, worth a thousand dollars if he could get them to a federal marshal. He could hide them from the animals, then come back for them.

If he survived the *Jornada.*

Sam drank from the Tanks. Then, slowly, suffering from heat and exhaustion and pain, still bleeding from his broken nose, he started down the canyon, to bury Slocum and Werdann. He would spend the night at the Tanks. He would drink and rest. Then, in the morning, he would begin his long walk back to civilization.

Martin Cruz would not be surprised to see him.